May God bless you.
Janie Jordan

THE
MAKING OF A
NEW CREATURE

JANIE JORDAN

WESTBOW
PRESS®
A DIVISION OF THOMAS NELSON
& ZONDERVAN

This is a work of fiction. All of the characters, names, incidents, organizations, and dialogue in this novel are either the products of the author's imagination or are used fictitiously.

WestBow Press books may be ordered through booksellers or by contacting:

WestBow Press
A Division of Thomas Nelson & Zondervan
1663 Liberty Drive
Bloomington, IN 47403
www.westbowpress.com
844-714-3454

Cover artwork provided by H.M. Hendrix aka Mike Hendrix used by permission. Images are of Mike Hendrix's own drawings used to illustrate Heaven and Hell.

Scripture taken from the King James Version of the Bible.

ISBN: 978-1-6642-1348-7 (sc)
ISBN: 978-1-6642-1350-0 (hc)
ISBN: 978-1-6642-1349-4 (e)

Library of Congress Control Number: 2020923122

Print information available on the last page.

WestBow Press rev. date: 12/02/2020

DEDICATION

I WOULD LIKE to dedicate this book to the many pastors in small churches who are still preaching the Gospel and helping people like Ken and Annie to know the Lord Jesus Christ. May God bless them.

ACKNOWLEDGMENTS

THIS BOOK WAS written because God told me to write it through a dream. I acknowledge Jesus Christ as my Savior and Lord so I try to listen to what he tells me. When I woke up from the dream God said to me, "Write it down." You will find that dream at the beginning of this book. He further instructed me as I sat down and wrote the book in two days. Naturally, it took longer to enter it in the computer. As I looked for a publisher, I found that it is not an easy job. When I found Westbow Press on the internet, I called and talked to a lady who explained everything to me from start to finish. Each person I have worked with at Westbow Press has been kind and gracious to a lady who knew very little about publishing a book.

Joannie Deneve, who has had three books published, previewed the first chapter for me. When I asked her if the first chapter would make her want to read the rest of the book she said, "Yes, I am pulling for you." It was a great encouragement to me.

My daughter-in-law, Dawn Jordan, helped me with understanding some of the technology with which I was not familiar. Thank you Dawn; you were a blessing.

The publisher sent me to a website with hundreds of pictures to look through for a front cover. I could not find a picture that suited the story. I prayed about it and woke up the next morning with God saying, "You already have the picture." I then remembered a picture my husband bought. He thought it was an exact picture of who he was before he became a Christian. After much time and patience I finally found H. M. Hendrix, the artist. As soon as he got a letter I sent, he called me and said, "This is Mike Hendrix and of course you can use my picture." He told me it was painted in 1977 and the man was a self-portrait of himself. It was great to meet Mike and his wife Brenda on the phone and I hope to meet in person someday. He and his wife were great encouragers to me.

When it was time to edit the book, the Lord reminded me of my granddaughter Rachel's husband, Matthew Byrne, who worked at a book company. He graciously said he would edit the book. He was a tremendous help to me. I can't thank him enough.

My friend and encourager, Pam Besteder, was my soul-winning partner for several years. When I mentioned the book and my doubts about publishing it to her, she said, "What was your first statement to me about the book?"

I said, "God told me to write it." I didn't have any doubts after that statement.

CHAPTER 1

ANNIE WOKE UP from her dream with the sound of the alarm clock; it was five-thirty in the morning and she must hurry. She never remembered her dreams, but this time it was so vivid, and so real. She was trembling and afraid; the dream had brought out a very real fear that her husband had been unfaithful to her. She had no evidence of it—just this fear.

Ken was not interested in horses unless they were under the hood of a hot-rod car, but in the dream he was with some of his drinking buddies and their girlfriends going horseback riding. They badgered Ken until he agreed to go along. A new girl was there whom Ken recognized as the barmaid at the local tavern. When they got back from the ride, everyone got in their cars to go home, but the barmaid had no way to get home. Ken was left as the others hurried in their cars. Ken took her home in his car. In the dream Annie saw where Ken pulled off the road and parked the car in a wooded area. He opened the door to get out of the car and Annie woke up. Annie's suspicions had entered her dreams.

Annie got out of bed, woke Ken, and went to the kitchen. She put the percolator coffeepot on and started Ken's breakfast. She packed a lunch for him to take to the Air Force Base. As she worked she thought, *How did I get to this place in my life?* They had been married since 1957. That was just five years ago, and she did not feel secure at all in her marriage. On top of working a full-time factory job, taking care of their two children kept her so busy and tired. She left the house for work at four in the afternoon and did not get home until after midnight. Not much sleep to start another busy day.

Ken came into the kitchen and sat down to drink his second cup of coffee. Annie had taken the first cup to him as soon as it was ready, just as she did every morning before he got up. She sat his eggs and grits in front of him along with a piece of toast. As he ate his breakfast Annie sipped a cup of coffee.

"I have to leave or I will be late." He bent over to kiss her goodbye. She stood up and hugged him real hard, and he kissed her again.

"Annie, you are really getting skinny."

"Nothing I can do about that. Working nights and taking care of the home in the day wears the pounds off me."

"See you around four. I'll take the motorcycle today. You can use the car if you need to run any errands."

"Thanks, but I doubt I will have time to run errands. I love you."

"Bye," Ken said as he rushed out the door.

Annie heard baby Sarah crying. She ran and changed her diaper. She laid her down in Annie and Ken's bed to nurse her. When Sarah went back to sleep, Annie fell off to sleep herself. Around nine Kenny Jr. woke her up with some peaches in the bed. He was just two years old but he knew how to get into the refrigerator. He had woken up hungry and got a bag of peaches. He brought them to Annie to open the bag for him. All the commotion in the bed woke baby Sarah. Sarah was three months old now. Annie went to work when she was two weeks old. She hated leaving the children but her husband's paycheck from the service just didn't stretch for all the bills. One night when she went to fix supper, there was nothing to eat but eggs. She scrambled them for her and Kenny and made some toast. Ken was at the gas station with his buddies. That was the day she decided to take a job at the factory, which was seasonal work that lasted three or four months. She would be laid off in another month. The job, nursing Sarah, and housework had led to her weighing ten pounds lighter than before her pregnancies. She knew she was skinny and tried to eat. She took a lunch to work, but she was just working off more than she was eating.

After getting Kenny a plate of eggs to go with his peaches, she ate some herself. She left Kenny in the highchair and nursed Sarah once more, laying her in the crib to sleep.

"Okay, Kenny, I am going to the laundry room to wash Sarah's diapers. You can play in there with your toy truck."

She dumped the dirty diapers in the laundry sink, rinsed the urine out of them, and then put them in the wringer washer. While the agitator moved the suds through the diapers, Annie ran a tub of rinse water. She got the laundry basket and checked on Sarah to see if she was still sleeping. She put the diapers through the wringer into the rinse water. She put the hose of the washer in the drain to let the dirty water out. She never washed clothes after the diapers. Since she slept in that morning, she didn't have time to do Ken's fatigues or other laundry. She put the rinsed diapers through the wringer and they fell into the basket on the floor.

"Okay, Kenny, let's go downstairs and hang the diapers on the line."

"Oh goody, outside, outside."

"Take my hand going down the steps, and be very careful."

"Yes, Mama."

The neighbor, Myrtle, was also hanging clothes in her yard. Annie got through hanging the diapers and walked to the fence.

"Hi Myrtle, how are you doing?"

"Oh, I am great; I know you must be tired with working and taking care of the two kids."

"Hopefully it will only be a few more weeks."

"You don't have to worry about the children; Rebecca takes good care of them when Ken goes to the station. She puts the baby in the baby buggy and pushes her around and takes Kenny for a walk."

Annie's mind whirled. Rebecca was the teenage girl that had babysat for her one day, for a couple hours. *What was she doing with my children at night when I was working?* Annie did not want Myrtle to know that was news to her.

"Myrtle, what time does Rebecca get here?"

"Her brother drops her off around five, just before Ken leaves, and picks her up around nine or ten."

Myrtle's living room and kitchen window looked out on Ken and Annie's driveway. She often knew what was going on in their yard.

"I need to get back in and check on the baby. Have a good day, Myrtle."

"You too, Annie."

How could Ken do this and not even tell me? she thought to herself.

CHAPTER 2

KEN HAD AGREED to watch the two children, which was the only reason Annie said she'd go to work at the cannery. Now he had hired Rebecca to babysit so he could do his thing. Whatever that was, it was unknown to Annie. She was so embarrassed that her neighbor and probably the whole town knew that Ken had hired Rebecca to babysit, but she did not know it. Everyone knew each other's business in their small town. The town was about two blocks long and the gas station was at the end of the block. She had taken the night shift—which was extremely hard on a new mother nursing a baby—just so Ken would be home with the children. Those babies were precious to her and she would not leave them if there were a way around it.

Annie and Ken did not have a phone, so she went downstairs to the store and used the payphone to call her supervisor. A telephone was something they could not afford.

"Sally, I am going to be a little late for work; I have to check on a babysitter for my children."

"You won't be long, will you? We need you on the packing line."

"I will try to not be over an hour."

"Well, okay. Don't forget rubber gloves. We are packing hot peppers tonight."

"Thanks for reminding me. See you later."

As she hung up the phone, Kenny said, "Candy, Mama."

"Just a minute, Kenny. Janis, do you have any rubber gloves in the store?"

Janis gestured to the right, where Annie saw some good latex gloves, which she purchased. She said, "Please give Kenny a sucker."

Kenny picked out a red sucker.

"Wait until after supper," Annie reminded him.

"That will be a dollar for the gloves and a penny for the sucker," Janis said.

"Here it is. I must hurry home and get Ken's supper ready before I go to work."

She went to the back yard and got the diapers down. She took them and Kenny up the stairs.

She sat down and folded the diapers. She dreaded packing the hot peppers. The gloves would work tonight but to use them the second night would mean her hands would burn. "I don't know how anyone eats those things. If they are doing to their stomachs what they do to my hands, their stomachs must be red hot," she said to Kenny, who was playing with his toys.

The dream she had that morning and the news from Myrtle about the babysitter had Annie very upset. She sat down with her Bible to calm herself down. In Psalms 61:1–2, she read, "Hear my cry, O God; attend unto my prayer. From the end of the earth will I cry unto thee, when my heart is overwhelmed: lead me to the rock that is higher than I?"

Annie prayed, "O God I feel all alone and don't know what to do; I am overwhelmed. The nurturing of my children versus the need to help support them is so present with me. Give me the right direction to talk to Ken. I don't want to fight with him. You know, God, how I vowed to you that I would not treat my husband like my mother treated my father. She screamed at him almost nightly. I know that is not what you want, so please help me show Ken my heart about this. Thank you Lord. Amen."

Annie did not want her children raised in the atmosphere she was raised in. Annie spent most of her time as a child at her grandma's, where she was taught about love and kindness. She did not remember any kind of loving from her mother. She was so thankful for her dad's mother, who was just the opposite. Ken came from a family with eight children and knew how to take care of little ones. Annie felt secure with him caring for the children.

She went to the kitchen and made a lunch to take to work. As she thought of supper, she mused, *Ken likes bacon, lettuce, and tomato sandwiches, so I think I will make him a couple of them and Kenny some macaroni and cheese.* She fried the bacon, cut the tomatoes and lettuce, and laid them on a small plate as she fixed the macaroni and cheese.

As she finished that, she ran to the bedroom to get her work clothes on. She picked up Sarah, changed her diapers, gave her a big hug, and sat down to nurse her. "If I didn't nurse you, Sarah, I would never get any rest. When I get to Heaven the Lord is going to have a bed waiting for me." Sarah cooed so sweetly. Annie put Sarah back in her bed and went to the kitchen to make a bottle of Similac baby formula for the bedtime feeding. She boiled the water and added the powder and put the bottle in the refrigerator. Annie nursed Sarah all the time, except this one bottle at night while she was working.

She put some bread in the toaster for the sandwiches as she heard Ken's motorcycle coming around the three big curves coming into town about a mile away. You could hear his motorcycle when he got to the first curve. He always went fast, townsfolk watching a lot of times to see if he made it around that last curve.

Ken came in the door and kissed her hello. She pulled away sooner than she usually did.

"What's wrong, honey?" Ken asked as he looked at her eyes, which were watering up with tears.

"Myrtle mentioned how well Rebecca was taking care of the children, taking them out for walks."

"Oh … that."

"Yes, that. How could you hire someone to babysit and not tell me about it? Do you know how keeping that a secret from me embarrassed me? I didn't let Myrtle know I was not aware of it. It made me feel like you do not care about me."

"I'm sorry I hurt you, but I had to go work on some cars for Randy at the gas station. Rebecca's brother was there one night when I had taken the kids in the baby buggy to the gas station with me. He volunteered to get his sister, so I said sure. I am only two blocks away if she needs me."

"How long has she been babysitting?"

"About a month."

"You mean to tell me you hired a babysitter a month ago to watch my babies? You know I really only left them to go to work because their dad was with them. What about Friday nights when the gas station closes early? Why does Rebecca come then?"

"She came the first Friday so I just went to the bar to have a few beers with the guys; I pay her out of the money I get for working on cars. I pay her fifty cents an hour."

Annie burst into tears and ran into the bathroom. Before she married Ken, she told him she did not want anything to do with alcoholic beverages and he agreed that was all right with him. She knew he probably had drinks with his buddies at the gas station, but this was too much. She remembered the first year they were married he brought a carton of beer home. His G.I. buddies were coming over to play pinochle that night. Annie saw the beer in the refrigerator and pitched it out the back door. Ken had never brought it in again. She fixed cookies or homemade chocolate pie and coffee for the single G.I. buddies who came to play cards. They enjoyed that just as much; it was like a touch of home.

She dried her tears and put her hair in a ponytail. She came out of the bathroom and Ken said, "I'll stay here on Friday nights; you are going to be late for work."

"I called my supervisor and told her I would be late because I had to talk to the babysitter. Sit down and eat your supper with Kenny. I hear someone coming up the stairs, so it must be Rebecca."

Annie opened the door and said, "Come on in Rebecca. I thank you for watching the children. Have you had any problems with them?"

"Not really. Kenny helps me locate things if I need them. Mr. Jenkins gives Kenny his supper, so I just clean up the kitchen and then take them for a walk. By then it is time for Kenny's bath and Sarah is ready for her bottle. After I burp her she goes right to sleep. Kenny goes to sleep pretty much after I put his pajamas on and read him a story."

"It sounds like you have done a good job. My husband tells me you have had a lot of experience with small children."

Rebecca smiled. "Yes, I am the second in a family of seven so I have had a lot of experience."

"Thank you, Rebecca, for taking good care of them. From now on you won't have to work on Friday nights. My husband will be doing that, so your brother does not have to bring you on Fridays."

"That's great; I have wanted to go to the football games on Friday nights."

Annie kissed the baby and Kenny goodbye. Ken walked her out to the car, kissed her, and got on his motorcycle. As he took off for the gas station, Annie wondered if he would ever become the man she thought she married. Nothing resolved, Ken once more had explained away her complaints.

As she got in the car, Ken's friend Jack drove up to the store and came over to say, "Hello Mrs. Ken. You sure have a cool husband."

"Oh? What has my cool husband done now?"

Jack chuckled. "I just mean the way he can rock back and forth with his feet behind his head when he gets a couple beers in him."

"Oh? When did you see that happen?"

"Thursday night at the bar."

"Have a good night, Jack."

She started the car and drove off. *So he was at the bar Thursday night too.*

CHAPTER 3

AS ANNIE DROVE the ten miles to work, she remembered what her preacher counseled her in Pennsylvania before she married Ken. "Don't marry Ken; you will regret it because the Bible tells us not to be unequally yoked with unbelievers. A Christian cannot marry an unsaved person. There will be much trouble."

Ken had been raised in a very strict cult, but he said he didn't believe in it. His mother sent elders from the church everywhere they moved to visit them. Ken would exit through the back door when he saw them coming. Annie was well versed in that religion because her preacher had taught a class on the cults when she was a teenager. She would let them say their rehearsed spiel and then give them her testimony about becoming a born-again Christian. They would return a couple of times and then give up.

She thanked the Lord once more that she had become a born-again Christian when she was twelve years old at a vacation bible school class. A neighbor took her and her sister to Sunday school at a little United Presbyterian church in Pennsylvania. A neighbor who lived closer picked them up also. She went every time the doors were opened. The youth leader's mom and dad would give them a ride on Sunday night to go to teen meetings. Sometimes the teen group went to different churches in the area for meetings. She loved the meetings and got very excited about following the Lord. She was very grateful for all those people who taught her about the Lord. Annie's parents were not Christians and when she told her mother she received the Lord into her heart and was born again, her mother said, "You always thought you were better than the rest of us." Annie did not understand the reaction but figured it must have to do with going to Grandma's so much. She was on her own when it came to church, then and now. Ken had gone to church with her before they were married. She asked him one time why he went with her before they were married and now wouldn't even after promising her he would. He replied, "I had not landed you yet. I had to do what you wanted to get you to marry me."

She had been proposed to twice and turned them down when she was only seventeen. Why did she marry Ken? She had prayed to God often to send a man that needed her to love him. She never felt like she had met anyone quite like that before Ken came along. She had loved him with all her heart and still did.

She wanted her children to be raised knowing the Lord and that the church was a good place. She took Kenny to Sunday school and he went in the nursery for church services. Ken kept baby Sarah and he watched car racing or football on the black-and-white nineteen-inch TV. Ken was good with Sarah. He could make her coo and laugh so easily.

"Oh, Lord, help me!" she cried as she pulled in the parking lot at work. She dried her eyes. *One thing I know—I will not have any more children to bring up in a home where the father is not saved. I will get some kind of birth control when I go for my six-week checkup next week. I am not sure about the new pills they have out. Women have headaches with them. I will ask the doctor.*

Annie had thought of leaving Ken several times but her deep love for him gave her a forgiving heart. Besides, where could she go and support the two children? The Bible does not allow for divorce. Despite his faults Annie loved him with all her heart. Because of that, it made the lying to her even more painful. When she looked in the Bible for an answer, it would bring her to Matthew 18:21–22. "Then came Peter to him, and said, Lord, how oft shall my brother sin against me, and I forgive him? Till seven times? Jesus saith unto him, I say not unto thee Until seven times: but, Until seventy times seven."

She put her hairnet on and got her rubber gloves, went in the cannery door, and punched the time clock. She was one hour late. That would be a dollar off her paycheck, since minimum wage was a dollar an hour. Only a few more weeks and she would be laid off from this seasonal work and she could collect $23 a week in unemployment.

That Saturday Annie did not have to work so she cleaned the house thoroughly and was going to start Ken's supper when he came into the kitchen and said, "We are going out tonight. Myrtle will watch the kids for a couple hours."

"Where are we going?"

"It's a surprise."

She fixed Kenny a grilled cheese sandwich and some tomato soup, nursed Sarah, took a quick shower, and put on clean clothes.

"Okay, I'm ready."

"You look beautiful as usual. I took the kids to Myrtle."

Ken drove a block away and said, "Here we are. I got to thinking this week; if you went to the bar with me, you would see how harmless it is."

"You know I don't want to go in there. I never go in a restaurant that sells liquor, much less a bar."

"Give it a try, please."

Annie went along with Ken; she noticed there were mostly men in the bar. Ken picked out a table for two and the waitress came over and said, "What do you want to drink, Ken?"

"We will have two beers."

Annie interrupted. "That will be one beer and a ginger ale."

The waitress gave Ken a little smile and left. When she brought the drinks back, Ken took a sip and put the glass down. Annie sat there looking around, sipping on her ginger ale. It was early and there were not many customers.

Ken said, "How do you know you don't like beer without taking a taste?"

Annie took a small sip of Ken's beer and made a terrible face.

"That is the most bitter and awful tasting stuff I ever tasted. Why in the world do people drink it? It's disgusting."

She took a sip of ginger ale to get the taste out of her mouth.

Ken said, "Okay, let's go."

"You haven't had but one sip of your beer."

"I can't drink it with you watching. Come on, I will take you to get some burgers in the city," he said as he laid a dollar bill on the table to pay for the drinks.

"I am sorry, Ken. I spoiled your plans, but I do not drink alcoholic beverages. Even if I did like them, it is not what Jesus Christ would want me to do. You did tell me before we got married you would not drink, but I know you do every chance you get. I resent me having to work to put groceries on the table, but you have money to spend on drinking. I love you and obey you as I promised in my wedding vows, but God's Word tells me to stay away from alcohol. I won't compromise, and I will pray that God shows you the right way."

Ken did not say anything until they got to the diner that had the biggest burgers in town. They went in and both ordered a cheeseburger. Ken put two nickels in the jukebox and one of his favorite Elvis tunes played: "I'm All Shook Up." He started singing the song as he came back to the table. Annie knew this was his way of communicating love to her. Then "Love Letters in the Sand" came on, a song by Pat Boone. Although Ken was a big Elvis fan, Annie preferred Pat Boone's type of music. Pat Boone identified as a Christian and his songs were softer and more loving than Elvis's. Although Elvis Presley did have some that were very sweet. Ken had played this one for Annie.

Annie said, "You can sing better than both of them."

When they finished eating, as they went to the car, Ken took Annie in his arms and gave her a big kiss just before getting in the car.

"I'm sorry for taking you to the bar. Am I forgiven?"

"You are. I enjoyed having the burger with you even if I couldn't eat it all. This was a special treat; we never go out to eat."

Annie got into the car and slid over to Ken and he put his arm around her as they drove home. She missed this terribly.

CHAPTER 4

LIFE GOES ON. After two years working at the canneries, Annie took an accounting course at the junior college nearby. A friend told her about a job at an optometrist's office. She applied and got the job. Ken had quit the military service after ten years and they all moved to Georgia where his family lived so that Ken could work in construction with his dad. After many problems, Ken decided to go back to the little town in Michigan. Annie always felt Ken was trying to get approval from his dad. It had been very hard pleasing his dad in his growing-up days.

Annie's commitment to God and her marriage kept her on her knees and in her Bible. She had developed friends in the church that were a blessing to her. A new preacher at the local church could really preach the scriptures well. Becky was a close friend with whom she loved to discuss the scriptures. Annie asked her to pray for Ken to be saved but did not divulge their home life. She felt that was too private to share.

The split in friends was very noticeable. Ken had friends who drank and liked cars and racing. Annie went with Ken to the Mt. Clemens speedway when Kenny was a baby but that track had closed down. Annie very seldom came in contact with his friends, and when she did they called her Mrs. Ken.

Ken loved to read, as did Annie. They had joined a book club a few years back. They got five books for ninety-nine cents to start and then a book a month for various prices. They had also bought a set of encyclopedias and children's storybooks they paid on by the month.

Ken's love for Elvis's music prompted him to join the record of the month club. They got a similar deal. They got five long-play albums to start and then each month a new record. They had collected a lot of the big band records and, of course, all of Elvis's long-play albums also. Sometimes Annie would ask Ken to dance with her. He always said, "You don't want to dance; you just want me to hold you in my arms, because you know I can't help myself from kissing you."

Ken took them some Saturday nights to the drive-in theater in town. They saw every Elvis movie that came out. Annie made popcorn to take with them. The kids loved going to the movies. She had them get their baths and wear pajamas so when they fell asleep, which they always did on the way home, they would be ready for bed when they arrived.

"It is Saturday; do you want to take us to the movies, Ken?"

"No, I am not in the mood. I am going to George's next door; there is a Euchre party," he said as he went out the back door. "See you later."

Annie cleaned up the kitchen, got the children ready for bed, read them a story, and listened to their prayers. She got the children's clothes ready for church in the morning. Ken had been gone almost two hours. The kids were asleep and she decided to go find out what the party was all about. She could hear the noisy music next door. George let her in and she saw Ken sitting at a card table playing Euchre. Everyone had a drink next to them but Ken had a soft drink. She recognized some of the people that lived around the area, men and women all drinking and talking loudly to be heard above the loud music. She was offered a drink and declined.

She walked over and watched Ken play awhile and then she said to him, so that everyone could hear, "I have something waiting for you at home you don't want to miss." Then she leaned down and whispered in his ear, "Fresh homemade fudge."

Everyone made hooting noises and George said, "Wow, Ken, I think you have a good deal going there."

"I'll be home at the end of this game," he said without looking up at her like he was annoyed with her checking up on him.

Putting on a fake smile, Annie went out the door, saying goodbye to everyone with a wave of her hand. She wanted to get out of there before she cried.

When Ken came home thirty minutes later she fixed him a plate of fudge and a glass of sweet tea. He ate some and sat at the kitchen table and played solitaire. He did that when he didn't want to talk to her because something was bothering him. Annie's attempt to get him away from his friends did not work. She knew he was unhappy with his work. His boss was taking advantage of his work ethic and paid him very little. Since he had gotten out of the service he had worked for three different people. When she tried to encourage him about his work, he clammed up and kept it to himself.

Annie had worked at the optometrist's three years now; he had paid her a dollar an hour to start and gave her a dollar raise every year. The kids were in school now so the pain of leaving them was not so bad. She had adjusted. A neighbor got the kids from the bus stop and watched them until she got home from work.

The loneliness was hard. She felt it because she and her husband lived separate lives even though they ate and went to bed together. Their hearts were not knit together. Annie wanted to share her Lord with a man who had thoughts of God. Ken would not talk about his problems so Annie was left out.

As she watched him play solitaire she thought back to the day they met. Annie went around the table and gave him a shoulder hug and teased, "Do you remember the day we met?"

She finally got a smile from him. "You know I do. Love at first sight." He continued playing cards. "I came to your town with your best friend's brother from the base one weekend in Pennsylvania. Bob said he had to go pick up Sis and her friend Rachel at the swimming place at the creek. It was a pretty June day, 1956. Bob parked about fifty yards from the creek and told me he was going to change into swimming trunks. 'You can go on down and meet Rachel, but you won't get anywhere with her. She won't date me at all.'"

Annie interrupted and said, "Bob was my best friend's brother, but I didn't trust him enough to go out with him alone. His reputation with the girls preceded him. I did get him to take me and Sis roller skating a couple times before he figured out that I wouldn't go out with him alone. However, I did teach him the two-step dance so he could go to his senior prom."

Ken had finished the card game. He pushed his chair back from the table and faced Annie and said, "I walked down that path going to the creek and saw Sis there with a girl with long red hair. As I got closer, I noticed she didn't have any freckles on her face. I never saw a redhead without freckles on her face. Then, when you came out of the water, I noticed you had more than red hair going for you. You looked like a beauty queen coming out of that water. I said to myself, 'I am going to marry that girl.'"

Annie sat on his knee and smiled, "You never told me you asked me to marry you because I didn't have freckles on my face. I know I was very impressed with that tall, dark, handsome stranger with muscles all over his body. I had no idea I would marry him though. I had turned down the guy's marriage proposal who took me to the junior/senior prom just a couple weeks prior to meeting you. I told him I was sorry, but I just didn't love him. Marriage was the last thing on my mind. I was only seventeen."

"You let me brush that long red hair when you got out of the water," Ken said as he stroked Annie's hair. "You don't know what that meant to me."

"My two brothers walked to the creek, stayed awhile swimming, and needed a ride home, so I got a little acquainted with you while we waited on them. Found out you were a nineteen-year-old Southern boy from Georgia. You had seven brothers and sisters. It sounded to me like you missed them. When I got in Bob's '49 Mercury Coupe to go home, I was the last one in, and when I raised the front seat to scoot in the back there was nowhere to sit but on your knee. I suspect that was you and Bob's doings."

"I put my arm around you to keep you from falling around the curves. My heart was pounding."

"Bob had adjusted his mirror to watch the back seat and I saw him grinning at us. He still takes credit for us getting married," Annie said, smiling at Ken.

"We dropped your brothers off and you grabbed some clothes so you could go to church with Sis that night. When we got to Bob and Sis's house everyone started getting out of the car and I grabbed your arm and said, 'Stay.' You did."

"I felt like you were a very lonesome military guy and I stayed to talk. Next thing I knew you put your hands on each side of my head and pulled me down to kiss me. Wow! I had kissed guys before but none was as precious as that kiss. We had the chemistry from the beginning."

Ken continued. "Then we kissed some more. Bob's mom came out to the car to invite us in the house. I asked her if she thought it was all right for us to get married. She said, 'If you both agree, I guess it's all right.'"

"I had no idea you were serious until I received a letter the next week from you saying you had asked your commanding officer's permission to get married. You brought the permission paper the next weekend when you came home with Bob. You came every weekend after that and I told you I was only seventeen and had a year to finish high school. I couldn't marry you. That was about the time you started calling me Annie. My whole name was Rachel Ann Johnson. Now I am Mrs. Annie Jenkins."

"Labor Day weekend was the last time I got to see you before I had to leave you, because I got my orders for Korea. I remember we went to Idora Amusement Park and had a great time together. We got pictures taken together by putting a quarter in one of those machines. I still carry one of them in my wallet. I took it to Korea with me and got a South Korean man to paint a picture of us. I told him the colors to put on the picture since the snapshot was black and white. He did a marvelous job."

"I was so thrilled when I got that in the mail from you; it was a precious gift."

"That was a hard thing to do, leaving you behind. Those three months we got acquainted with each other showed me I had to make you my wife. I would never meet anyone as beautiful as you, and when I held you in my arms, you made my blood boil. I wanted so much more, but you said no."

"That is one of the reasons I loved and respected you, because when I said no, you backed off. I didn't want to lose you either."

"Your letters kept me going. You sent two or three a week. They made me happy at every mail call. The guys in the barracks wanted me to read the letters to them. When you sent a picture, you would think you were their girlfriend too. Then finally the day came when I got my orders to go home. That was a long year."

"It wasn't so long for me because I was going to school and I got

THE MAKING OF A NEW CREATURE

that part-time job at the dairy bar as a carhop. I worked after school from five to nine every night and Friday and Saturday until midnight."

"I got orders for Florida and you were in Pennsylvania so I asked you to come to Georgia and meet my family. We got married in Georgia before we went on to Florida."

"I never will forget the look on your face when I stepped off that train in Georgia with two Navy guys. I explained to you right away and introduced you to them. I was eighteen, riding on my first train. I made it fine, even changing trains in Cincinnati. When I got settled in my seat, an older man got on and sat in the seat across from me. There weren't a lot of people on the train so I just sat in a seat by myself and so did he. After a while he started unzipping his pants. I turned my face away so I couldn't see him and I saw his reflection in the train window because it was dark outside. I was scared and just praying the conductor would come through but he didn't. I shut my eyes and laid my head back."

Annie continued, "Two sailors came up from behind me. They apparently saw what was going on. One of them came and sat with me and the other went and sat with the old man. I was thankful; I wasn't scared of them. Since they were military I knew I could trust them. The one who sat with me asked where I was going. I told him about you. He told me they were on their way to Pensacola where they would ship out. He told me about his girlfriend and hoped she waited on him like I did for you because he would be gone a year or so. It made the rest of the trip go fast. They offered to carry my suitcases off the train. They were perfect gentlemen."

Ken said, "I must admit I was a little anxious for a minute when I saw them carrying your suitcases off the train. I knew when I got you in Dad's old Packard and got that first kiss from you I had nothing to worry about."

"Oh, yes, the butterflies were still there." Annie smiled at Ken.

"I'm glad you married me and have stayed with me. I don't deserve you." Then Ken put his hands in Annie's hair and pulled her face down for one of those kisses she loved so much.

"I still love you just as much if not more than I did then. Still get the butterflies when you kiss me," Annie said.

"I hope you always will," Ken replied.

CHAPTER 5

THE NEXT MORNING, as Annie and the two children were ready for church, she asked one more time. "Ken, won't you come to church with us?"

He shook his head no and looked at her intently.

"Are you ashamed of me?" she asked.

"I never could be ashamed of you," he replied as he kissed her goodbye.

The church was less than a block away. As she walked with the children to church, she noticed the new pastor and his wife and two children coming out of the parsonage. "Look, the new pastor and his wife are right ahead of us. They have Charlie and Theresa with them."

"Can we play with the kids after church, pleeezz?" begged Kenny.

"We will see what the Wests have planned; maybe the kids can come over after lunch and play in our yard."

"Oh goody," Sarah said excitedly.

Charlie and Theresa were the same ages as Kenny and Sarah. Pastor West had graduated from Moody Bible Institute a few years prior to coming to this country church in Michigan. His wife Mary was quiet but friendly, with a pretty smile—a new friend for Annie, she hoped. He knew his Bible well, and Annie appreciated the good sermons. They were encouraging to her. She loved hearing the Word of God preached.

She had a good background of Bible from the church she went to as a teenager. Although she had no help at home from her parents to live a Christian life, she had a godly pastor who was an excellent Bible teacher. She heard him preach several times, "Ye must be born again." She had trusted the Lord to save her at twelve years old at a vacation bible school class.

The youth group at her church was inspirational and fun to attend. The leader of the youth was a senior in high school and had surrendered to preach. He went to Bible college after graduating. She was encouraged to enter Bible reading contests and went to summer camp. She learned from these godly people about how to live a Christian life. She longed to have a Christian home. She joined a youth choir of area churches for Easter and loved singing the great hymns of the faith. The first hymn she sang in a choir was "'Wonderful Grace of Jesus," which had become her favorite hymn.

The first two years they were married she did not go to church because Ken would not go. When Kenny was born she realized she had to go by herself for her children's sake. Those two years when she didn't go to church she read her Bible from cover to cover. She marked the passages of Scripture that applied to her present problem. This helped her to follow the Lord even though her husband would not.

Many times she came across I Corinthians 7:10–16 and clung to the verses that told her to stay with her unbelieving husband, especially verse 16: "For what knowest thou, O wife whether thou shalt save thy husband." She believed God put that verse there for her benefit.

She also marked I Peter 3:1, "Likewise, ye wives, be in subjection to your own husbands; that, if any obey not the word, they also may without the word be won by the conversation of the wives." She learned the word conversation meant the way of your life. Not to preach to him, but live your life through Christ before him. She prayed each day that she could live Christ before Ken.

Going out of the church that day, Reverend West and his wife Mary were greeting people. Annie waited for everyone to leave so the kids could ask about playing after Sunday dinner. "Reverend West, I enjoyed that message. Mrs. West, that was a beautiful song you sang with your husband. Your voices blend very well."

"Thank you, Mrs. Jenkins."

"Please call me Annie; my friends do. My name is Rachel Ann, but Ken nicknamed me Annie and it stuck."

"Okay, Annie, call me Mary."

"Kenny and Sarah would like to know if Charlie and Theresa could come to our place after lunch and play. They will be playing outside; you can see our backyard from your house."

"Mary and I will talk about it and get back with you. By the way, I have been meaning to talk to you about a different teaching position. I know you are doing a great job with the junior-age children, but I think you can do more. Mary told me about the excellent lesson you taught the ladies last week at the ladies' fellowship. I have observed that you have a good Bible knowledge. We need a college-and-career-age class. I think you could teach it."

"Oh, Pastor, I don't know about teaching adults."

"It's just like teaching children except on a little higher level. I understand you have been going to the Michigan Sunday School Association's annual meeting in Detroit at Cobo Hall."

"Oh yes, I have learned so much from the great storyteller Ethel Barrett, and the preaching of Dr. V. G. Vick, and the Bourbon Street New Orleans preacher Bob Harrington, and the many workshops of great teachers. I heard Dr. W. A. Criswell tell us how important it is that we use the King James Bible as we teach. One of the quotes I wrote down and read over and over is 'To lift him up, to preach His name and to invite souls to love Him and to follow him is the highest, heavenliest privilege of human life.'"

"You certainly have heard some great teachers and preachers," Pastor West said. "I can tell you have a gift for teaching. Pray about it and let me know in the next few days. I am going to have some teacher training classes on Thursday nights while Mary teaches all the kids who come with the parents."

"Oh that would be great. I would love to come, if it is okay with Ken."

"Why does Ken not come to church?"

"He is not saved, but I have faith that God will save him soon. I am praying that way."

"Mary and I will be praying for his salvation also."

"Thank you both. I appreciate that so much."

"Okay, kids, let's go home."

"What's for Sunday dinner?" Kenny asked.

"Meatloaf and baked potatoes are in the oven."

"Oh boy, I love meatloaf." Kenny loved everything when he was hungry.

As they went in the door, she could smell the meatloaf. Ken was watching a football game on the television. She kissed Ken and gave him a hug and said, "The new pastor and his wife are such nice people. He really knows his Bible also. He asked me to teach a young-adult Sunday school class. I am not sure I can do it. I told him I would ask you if you think it is okay for me to do it."

"You know I would not stop you from doing something at the church within reason."

"He is starting a teacher training class on Thursday nights, which I would love to go to also."

"Well, I might be working on a truck at work and not be able to stay with the kids."

"Thursday night is the wrestling night on the TV and Leaping Larry Chene is always on. You like to watch them wrestle. I like to watch Larry Chene too. I don't care for that Dick the Bruiser, but you can enjoy them both. The class is for ten weeks, an hour a night, and his wife Mary will have a class for the kids who don't have anyone at home to watch them."

"When you look at me with those pretty green eyes and that puppy dog look, how could I refuse?"

She kissed him and said, "Thank you, honey; dinner will be on the table in a few minutes." It was important to Annie to ask Ken about doing new things. She wanted him to know she valued him as the boss in the house.

CHAPTER 6

ANNIE FOUND THAT teaching the young adult group was a challenge, but she enjoyed it. It kept her mind busy when Ken was working on cars late at night. The pastor gave all the Sunday school teachers a general outline to follow teaching the Gospel message of John. Annie prayed about ways she could make the class interesting as she taught them the outline: seven accounts of Jesus saying "I am," seven accounts of the seven miracles, and the seven eyewitness accounts of people who said Jesus was the Son of God. She made up scenarios like, "What would you do if someone told you Jesus was just a man?" She asked questions like, "Was Nicodemus saved in John Chapter 3?" She taught the class and pointed out in each chapter if one of the seven of the series appeared. Annie reviewed each chapter, pointing out in each lesson the fact that John wrote to prove Jesus was the Son of God.

When she taught the First Miracle she brought a bottle of grape juice to class and poured everyone a small cup to drink and proceeded to explain that the word wine in the Bible is often mistaken because the Greek word for wine is *oinos* meaning grape juice, grape jelly, or anything made from grapes. In Proverbs we are told not to drink wine when it is red or when it moves in the cup. We learn that the new wine is grape juice, not fermented juice (red wine) as many would like to believe.

At the end of that series of classes, Pastor West asked Annie to take part with him in a skit titled "The Trial of Jesus." Annie was the defense attorney to prove Jesus is the Son of God. Pastor West was the prosecutor to prove Jesus is not the Son of God. This play would be impromptu. Without any practice, it would be quite a challenge. Annie got seven people from the class to testify as the seven eyewitnesses who would be on the defense's side. Annie asked each one of the seven to improvise on the costume they wore.

The night came for the program and Annie asked Ken to go but he didn't want to attend. She explained it wasn't church, just a program, and that she had a big part in it. Ken reluctantly came and sat on the back row with Kenny and Sarah.

The judge called for opening statements.

The prosecution said, "We will prove Jesus is just a mortal man, not the Son of God."

Annie prepared an opening statement to read. "The Bible, especially the book of John, is not really on trial. It has proved itself. Rather the people who criticize it are on trial and their fault-finding attitudes reveal their ignorance of the nature of scripture and their spiritual inability to appreciate it.

"Nor is Jesus really on trial. What His enemies say about Him does not affect His person one iota. This travesty of justice with its prefabricated verdict was based on hatred rather than on a desire that justice be done. Tonight we will prove by the FACTS that Jesus is the Son of God."

Pastor West as the prosecutor called on the Chief Priest, Judas, Caiphas, and an anonymous Jewish leader. He pointed out with these witnesses the Jewish rules and that the Messiah, the Christ, was to be from Bethlehem, not Nazareth where Jesus was born. That Jesus couldn't even be a good Jew because He healed on the Sabbath. Annie's cross-examination went well proving otherwise.

Then it was the defense attorney's time. Annie had given her class a few preliminary questions she might ask each of the seven who would testify.

The first of the defense witnesses was called to the stand by the bailiff (one of the deacons) and took an oath, "Do you promise to tell the truth, the whole truth, and nothing but the truth?"

The first witness said, "I do." He was wearing some kind of fur wrapped around his neck and hanging down to his waist and had leather from a deer's hide wound around his waist. The audience clapped when they saw his outfit. He carried a platter with a jar of honey.

Annie was proud of this young college student who came up with exactly what he needed to show he was John the Baptist. She rose and walked up to him. "What is your name?" asked Annie.

"I am John the Baptist."

"Tell us how you know that Jesus is the Son of God," she continued.

"It was why I was born to be the forerunner for the Christ, the Son of God. I stayed in the desert in the wilderness and waited until God prompted me to baptize with water. I was at the River Jordan baptizing those who wanted to repent of their sins when this man, Jesus, came walking up; He is the Christ, the Son of God."

"That is all I have for this witness, Your Honor."

The judge was another one of the deacons dressed in a black choir robe.

"Prosecution, do you want to cross-examine this witness?"

Pastor jumped up and said, "I certainly do, Your Honor."

"Now, Mr. John the Baptist, you say this Jesus was the Son of God."

"I know He is the Son of God."

"How did you know out of the hundreds of people you baptized that this wasn't just another stranger?"

"I saw the Spirit descending from Heaven like a dove, and it abode upon Him. I didn't know who He was, but He that sent me to baptize with water, the same said unto me, upon whom thou shalt see the Spirit descending, and remaining on Him, the same is He which baptizeth with the Holy Ghost. And I saw, and bare record that this is the Son of God."

Annie called witness two, Nathaniel, who testified that Jesus saw him under a fig tree in a different city and Nathaniel cried out, "Rabbi, thou art the Son of God."

Then witness three, the woman of Samaria, testified. The bailiff said, "State your name."

"Rachel Ann Jenkins, but everyone calls me Annie." That broke up the audience as well as Annie. Pastor's wife Mary played the part and kept a straight face. It threw Annie by surprise and it took a while to get her composure back. Mary had used her name for the woman of Samaria in John chapter four who had many husbands and was not married to the man she was with now.

The woman of Samaria testified that Jesus told her everything she did. "Was He not the Christ?"

Witness four, Simon Peter, testified to the fact that Jesus had the words of eternal life. "And we believe and are sure thou art that Christ, the Son of the Living God."

Witness five, the blind man was dressed like a beggar very effectively. He said, "I told those Pharisees the truth. I was blind and after He spit on the ground and made clay; He anointed my eyes with the clay. He then told me to wash in the pool of Siloam. I did and I could see. Those Jewish rulers even went and asked my parents about that miracle. My parents just told them, 'He was born blind. We don't know how he can see now. He is of age; ask him.' They still wouldn't believe. I saw Jesus again and He asked me if I believed on the Son of God. I told Him to tell me who He was so that I could believe. He told me I had seen Him, and it is He that talks with me. I fell down and worshipped him and said, 'Lord I believe.'"

Witness six, Martha of Bethany, the sister of Mary and Lazarus, told of her eyewitness account of Jesus raising her brother from the dead after he was buried in the tomb five days. "I believe Jesus is the Christ, the Son of God."

Witness seven, Mary Magdalene, was probably the most effective witness, as she told of His crucifixion and the people who were at the cross and then how she saw Him at the tomb after He rose from the dead. She didn't recognize Him until He said her name and she said, "Master."

Of course the prosecution tried to cross-examine and accuse her of having seven demons, but she squelched that with, "I did have, but Jesus made me whole."

The closing argument given by the prosecution was similar to the first, bringing up historians who did not believe Jesus was the Son of God.

Annie picked up her speech she wrote for the conclusion.

"Ladies and gentlemen, we could sum up our case with many facts, but we will stick to just the few we presented to you tonight, the seven eyewitness accounts that Jesus is the Son of God. Because man wants his own way, he ignores Jesus's life, works, and miracles. When man wants his own way rather than justice, he does not go out of his way to examine evidence that may prove him wrong. If Caiaphas and his Jewish friends had examined the facts, they would also say Jesus is the Son of God.

"Jesus was and still is the Son of God. He proved Himself by His miracles, by fulfilled prophecy, by His love for man, by His own statement, and by God's statement from Heaven.

"John says because God loved man so much, because man could not get out from under sin, God became man to show us a perfect life but more He showed us His love by going to the cross where He endured Hell for us, for our sin.

"The facts are here. Caiaphas, Judas, Pilate, and other Jewish leaders failed to see the facts, failed because they were too interested in themselves and what might be found out about their sin. If Jesus were really the Son of God, they knew they would be found to be thieves and irresponsible men in the high offices they held.

"Those who knew Christ gave you the facts: Jesus did do miracles, He did fulfill prophecy, and He did love man as God does. He did die on the cross for man and He did rise from the dead as He said He would.

"And most of all, He does live yet. He lives in the lives of every born-again Christian. We will see Him when we die and go to be with Him.

"The reason the priests and Pharisees did not believe is the same reason that man does not believe today: they don't read the facts in their Bibles. John wrote the facts that we might read and believe that Jesus truly is the Son of God."

Annie sat down and everyone clapped. The judge pounded his gavel and dismissed the witnesses.

Pastor called all the witnesses up to take a bow. Annie was very pleased with her class and told them so later in the evening.

"Annie, come up here and take a bow." Everyone clapped again. "For someone so young, it's hard to believe how well Annie knows her Bible."

Pastor West thanked everyone for coming and told them some

ladies had prepared refreshments. Pastor West closed in prayer, blessing the food.

Ken came up from the back and gave Annie a hug. "I didn't know you could speak that well. I am so proud of you."

"There are a lot of things you don't know about me; thank you for the compliment. Will you stay for refreshments with us?"

"Sure, I know a lot of these people."

"Have you met the pastor and his wife?"

"Yes, I was working on my car at the side of the house last week and they came over and introduced themselves to me."

"We won't stay long; the children need to be in bed soon for school tomorrow. The program was a lot longer than I thought. Then we didn't rehearse so I really had no idea how long it would be."

People came up congratulating Annie on a job well done. Annie looked at Ken; he just beamed when someone said something good about Annie.

CHAPTER 7

KEN WAS NOW working for a car dealer in the parts department. He would tell Annie about how he categorized the parts that were just lying around in boxes. There were hundreds of boxes full of parts from all different models of trucks and cars. He made shelves and labeled them and put the correct parts in each area of the shelves so labeled. This made everything easy to find. Ken was a perfectionist in his ways and manners, so this was a good project for him.

At home he always kept his clothes picked up and hanging in his closet and his shoes with their toes all pointing one way, as he was taught in the service. Annie made sure when she washed his clothes that they got hung up the way he liked them and that she folded his underclothes and put them in a drawer.

Ken told Annie when work got slow in the parts department that he would go to the back of the shop and see if he could help the mechanics out, which made him late coming home. With all he was putting into his job, Ken received no pay raises. His boss did not realize what a good worker Ken was. When he had been there a year Annie suggested he ask about a raise. Ken did and his boss told him maybe after he was there a few more years. Ken was very disappointed, but he loved working there. Ken stayed out many nights, just telling Annie he was working on a car or a truck with the mechanics.

It was Thursday night and Annie had just gotten in with the kids. They had been at the ETTA training at church. Evangelistic Teacher Training Association was the curriculum being used. Pastor West was teaching on the book, *Teaching Techniques*. Annie was enjoying so much learning how different techniques of teaching made the classroom more interesting for the pupils in Sunday school.

"Mrs. West said I did a good job on my lesson tonight," said Kenny.

"I am proud of you Kenny; that is good to hear. Sarah, how did your lesson go? Do you enjoy going to Mrs. West's class on Thursday nights?"

"Yes, Mama, I love it."

"Well kids, it is late and there is school tomorrow. Since you got your showers before you went to church you can get in your pj's and brush those teeth. I will be in to tuck you in shortly."

When she went to Kenny's room to tuck him in to go to bed, he asked his mama a question. "Why does Daddy not go to church with us?"

"Well Kenny, it's like this. When your dad was young like you, he did not go to a Sunday school and church like ours. He never learned he had to ask Jesus in his heart to be saved like you have done. When someone has Jesus in his heart, the Holy Spirit leads him to go to church and do right things. When he doesn't, he gets led astray by something else."

"You mean like the devil, don't you?"

"Yes, Kenny, but there is something we can do about it."

"But what can we do, Mama?"

"We can pray that Daddy gets saved soon."

"Can we pray tonight when I say my prayers?"

"Yes, and I will pray with you also."

As Kenny prayed his prayers, Annie noticed he prayed so earnestly that his daddy would be saved soon. Annie kissed him goodnight and turned out the light.

Annie got ready for bed and kneeled down and cried out, "Oh Lord, please help Kenny's prayer to be answered. I know that Ken has to come to the end of himself and realize he is a sinner. Please show him. Keep him safe until that day. He is a good man, Lord. Please, please help him."

It was way past the time Ken usually got home, even when he worked late. Annie was worried but had no way to call him. No one answered the phones after closing time. At last she heard his truck pull up at midnight. He came stumbling in the door and fell on the couch.

"Ken, what's the matter? Are you sick?"

"I am throwing up sick drunk. I never am going to take another drink." With that he ran to the bathroom, where Annie could hear him vomiting.

Annie had never seen Ken drunk before. He apparently could hold his liquor well. She could tell when he had been drinking because he had this happy-go-lucky attitude. This was different. He had done his best at getting Annie to like liquor. One time several years ago he had taken her out to eat for her birthday. He ordered some drinks. When they came, hers was pink. He told her it was cherry pop. She tasted it and could not tell that it was anything but cherry pop. After she drank about half of it, she felt dizzy. When she asked, he told her it was sloe gin. She pushed it away. It just ruined her evening.

Ken came out of the bathroom and went straight to bed and passed out. He never would tell Annie where he had been or what caused him to drink so much. Somehow he got up the next morning and gave Annie a kiss goodbye.

As he went out the door to go to work he said, "Annie, I am sorry. I will never drink again."

Ken started coming home earlier, only working a couple nights late. One Friday night he came in after work around six o'clock and said, "Annie, I am going down to Jake's house to help him change motors in his car. He has an old wrecked car with a better motor in it than the one in his car. I will be late, but I won't be drinking. He is going to help me with a project I have in the works. It will be a surprise."

Annie had fallen asleep and Ken woke her coming in the door. It was 5:00 a.m.

"Sorry to wake you; go back to sleep."

"Why so late getting in?"

Ken got in the bed beside her and gave her a big kiss. "We pulled the old motor out of Jake's car, pulled the new motor out of a wrecked car, and completely changed them. It took all night. We did it in Jake's dad's barn. You should hear the new motor purr like a kitten."

"Well, that's good; now get some sleep. I'll let you sleep in a while."

"Wake me by noon." Ken drifted off sound asleep.

Ken was in a good mood every night that week. He told Annie he would be late because Jake was helping him on his surprise. Annie knew Ken loved working on cars. He had done some different things with cars. He had bought a wrecked Starfire and taken it to Detroit to race at the drag strip. Annie learned this through one of his friends; it was some of those nights she did not know where he was. He was working on cars all right—racing cars. He had put a Packard motor in their '59 Edsel after burning the original motor up from hot-rodding it. He had told Annie it was the only thing that he could find to fix the Edsel. When she went to get in the car, the transmission was sitting in the front seat between the driver and passenger. Ken finally had to get rid of it after realizing it was a danger to anyone riding in the car. He also found a Chevy engine would fit into a Ford truck if you twisted and bent and pushed it in tight. He had put a Pontiac engine in the '55 Chevy they drove to San Antonio for TDY (Temporary Duty Yonder) in 1962 when he was in the service. Annie prayed all the way that they would make it.

Now, I wonder what his surprise is, thought Annie.

On Friday night Ken came in from work with a '65 Mustang.

"Surprise," said Ken. "This is what I have been working on. I traded my truck in for this Mustang. It had a dent in the door and needed to be painted. I borrowed the money from the bank to get it and paid for insurance on it. It has thirty-five thousand miles on it and it is only three years old. Isn't it a beauty?"

"Yes, it is very pretty, Ken. I am glad you are finished with it. You did a good job on the paint. There isn't a transmission in the front seat, is there?"

"Come and see. I'll take you for a spin around the block."

"Oh boy, can we go too?" Kenny said with glee.

"Sure, and after supper we will all go to the drive-in movie. Elvis's new movie *Speedway* is playing and it is only one dollar a carload on Friday nights."

"It is beautiful, Ken. I love it," said Annie when they got back to the house.

Then Ken broke out singing an Elvis song. "Get out in that kitchen and rattle those pots and pans."

"I have some sloppy joes already, so it won't take long to finish." Annie reached up and pulled Ken's face down and kissed him. "I am glad you are so happy tonight."

When Ken was happy he sang Elvis songs to Annie. He had a very good singing voice. Annie loved this man with all her heart and yet she knew he was missing something in his life that made him sad a lot of the time. It was good to see him so happy. That was what working on cars did for him. A lot of Ken's money went for working on cars, buying old ones and fixing them. He paid the sixty-dollar rent money each month, but Annie never saw any more of his pay. Making a car payment was going to cut his money down. Ken never worried about money. Annie worked and made a pretty good living so he had no idea of the expense of the children's clothing or food.

They all went to the drive-in that night and Ken stayed home Saturday washing and cleaning his new Mustang. Later that night he watched the Georgia Bulldogs play football on the television. He would always be a Southern man. Annie sat next to Ken on the couch to watch with him. He put his arm around her and smiled at her.

"You are such a good wife."

"I love you, my tall, dark, and handsome man."

"Oh, unreal."

CHAPTER 8

THE MUSTANG WAS a joy to Ken for a few months. He did not discuss his payments with Annie. She had her little Volkswagen she drove to work. It was four years old and ran well. Annie had found a widow, Mrs. Anderson, who only had to walk a block to come to Annie and Ken's apartment. She said she would get the children from the school bus and walk them home to put their books and lunch boxes in the apartment before they would go to her house. They got off the school bus at 3:30 p.m. and Annie got home by 5:30 p.m. so it was just a couple of hours until Annie got home from work. Mrs. Anderson was doing a great job of caring for the children.

Annie enjoyed a friendship with the pastor's wife and another Christian lady, Becky. She called Becky about once a week and they discussed some Bible promises. One of the promises they discussed was Psalm 37:4–5. "Delight thyself in the Lord; and he shall give thee the desires of thine heart, Commit thy way unto the Lord, Trust also in him; and he shall bring it to pass."

Annie mentioned to Becky and Mary that the desire of her heart was to see Ken saved. They were praying together after a ladies' meeting at church.

"I don't know what more I could do to trust in the Lord or to commit my way to the Lord. Why are my prayers not getting answered?" asked Annie to the two ladies.

"Maybe they are in a way," Mary replied.

"What do you mean?" asked Becky.

"Well, when a person gets saved they have to come to the end of their self, especially an adult who has walked in his sin for many years."

"Yes, Mary, like Pastor preached this past Sunday on sin. To be saved a person has to come to the place where they know that they are a sinner," said Annie. "So our prayers for Ken's salvation may have brought him to the place where he got drunk so bad he got sick and said he learned his lesson and would not drink anymore. Is that what you mean?"

"The burden on him that drinking was wrong probably didn't affect him as long as he drank a few beers and no harm came to him. God might have allowed him to be put in a place where he drank too much and became sick. Getting drunk showed him what he was doing was wrong. He changed himself not to do that anymore, but God still has to show him his sin for him to be saved," Mary answered.

Becky said, "We will continue praying for his salvation and that he realize his sin before God."

"Thank you, ladies."

Annie kept praying for Ken daily for his salvation.

Friday evening came. Annie got out of the car and walked the block to get the children from the sitter.

"Mrs. Anderson helped us make cookies today," said Kenny.

"Yes, and she gave us some in a bag. She said we had to wait until after supper to eat them," Sarah said.

"Mrs. Anderson is a sweet lady; she takes good care of you two. I would hate to leave you children with just anyone. Okay, let's get inside and I will fix supper."

Annie walked in her bedroom to change her uniform. She tried to take care of her three uniforms for work. She hung it up hoping she could wear it another day. She went to the dresser to get a blouse out and saw a note lying on the bed. She recognized Ken's handwriting. She read it out loud. "I can't stand it anymore. I have to leave." He didn't sign it.

She put her clothes on and walked out to the living-room window. Seeing Myrtle outside, she went out and walked over to the fence and asked, "Myrtle, did you see Ken today?"

"Yeah, he was here early this morning. I saw him leave again just a little before noon."

"Thanks Myrtle. Have a good weekend."

Annie was stunned while she walked back in the house. *He left at noon. He has been gone for six hours,* she thought as she walked back into the house. The kids were playing in their bedrooms so she quickly dialed Becky.

"Hello, Becky. I hate to bother you at suppertime, but I don't know what to do." She started crying.

"Never mind supper; what's wrong?"

She told Becky about the note and read it to her. She could hear the intake of Becky's breath. It had startled her also.

"Where did he go?"

"I have no idea."

"He will probably be back tomorrow. He may have just gone to a motel to be alone awhile or something. You will hear from him soon, I'm sure."

Becky then prayed for Annie and Ken.

Annie went about getting the children's supper. After cleaning up the kitchen she sent the children to get their baths.

"Will Daddy be home soon?" Kenny asked, coming out in his pajamas.

"Daddy has gone away on a business trip," Annie lied to them.

"Can we watch the Disney movie tonight and eat cookies and milk?" asked Sarah.

"That sounds good to me," replied Annie.

After the kids were tucked into bed, she went to bed and prayed for Ken's safety, and especially that he would call her and let her know what was wrong. She was baffled as to why he did this to her. What had she done? She cried herself to sleep.

Annie usually drove the ten miles to the city on Saturdays to buy groceries at Kroger or Kmart. She did not want to miss a call from Ken, so she decided she would get a few things she really needed at the country store nearby. It would cost more but she would adjust later. She had no idea how long she would be buying groceries for three instead of four. She waited until noon but needed milk and bread for the kids.

"I'll be right back, Kenny. Answer the phone if it rings."

She went in the store and the owner Janis was at the counter. Annie put the bread and milk on the counter and a dozen eggs.

"I haven't seen Ken's Mustang today," Janis said as she rang up the groceries.

"He has gone out of town," Annie replied.

"Will he be gone long?"

"I'm not sure how long he will be gone." Annie paid for the milk and bread. "Have a good day, Janis."

"Everybody in small towns knows all your business," Annie said to herself. "I wonder who all knows about Ken leaving, and if they know why, even if I don't." Annie tried not to panic.

"Kenny, did anyone call?" she asked as she put the groceries away.

Annie took the children to church the next day and spoke to Pastor West and Mary about Ken's leaving and about the short note he left. They promised to pray.

Sunday came and went. Monday morning Annie got up and saw the children off on the school bus and drove on to work. The only people she discussed this heartache with were Becky and the pastor and his wife. They promised they would not discuss it with anyone.

Ken, where are you? Why? Why? Why?

CHAPTER 9

ONE WEEK HAD passed and no word from Ken. People in town quit asking when Ken was coming home because they got Annie's pat answer: "I don't know." Annie tried to keep things as normal as possible during this time for the kids. She hid her feelings the best she could.

Each night she would read a book to the kids and listen to their prayers before tucking them in for bed. Each night Kenny, who was saved and would be nine years old in a couple weeks, prayed for his daddy to be saved.

Annie would get her shower and go to her bedroom. Praying for Ken was the first thing she did in the morning and the last thing she did at night. She tried to give the whole situation to God, but it was hard. She felt all alone in her turmoil. She continually asked herself questions like *Where is he? What have I done to chase him away?*

Ken had run away from something. She did not know what. It was a pattern he had gone through when he was a teenager. His home situation was so abusive that he couldn't stand it and had run away three times. Twice his dad found him and brought him home, but the third time he was sixteen and he let him stay in a small town where he worked in a garage and learned how to be a mechanic. Ken had taken Annie on their honeymoon to meet his former landlady who owned a boarding house where Ken had stayed the time that he was away from his home. He seemed so proud to introduce Annie to the landlady. The fact that Ken came from an abusive home made him into a man who hated violence and never lifted his hand against Annie.

Was he running from Annie, his kids, his job, or what? Maybe it was just God from whom he was running? There certainly had been a lot of prayer for his salvation in recent weeks by the pastor and his wife, Becky, and Annie. The first step in coming to know the Lord was conviction. Sometimes it was a hard thing for people to bear. She believed the episode with Ken's drunkenness was God letting him know how wrong it was to be a drinker of alcoholic beverages. It scared Ken into stopping. Annie never did hear from Ken why he got so drunk. He would not talk about it. As far as Annie knew he had not indulged since that night.

Sunday morning Pastor West titled his sermon "Choose God Against the World." He stated that a Christian can't escape the fact that God will remold him into a new creature.

The children were being a great help in keeping Annie from getting so lonely. As the second week started, Annie took them out to play with their friends every night until it started to get dark. There were several children about their age around the block they lived on. There were the pastor's two children, Charlie and Theresa; Myrtle's little seven-year-old boy; and two boys across the street at the corner. Annie was very careful to watch them because Kenny and Sarah loved to go across the street and play on the boys' swing set. The cars would come around that corner hot-rodding and she warned them to not cross the street without her. One time Kenny came running in the house saying Sarah had gotten hit with the swing across the street and was bleeding. Annie grabbed a towel and wet the end of it and ran across the yards to get to her. Sarah was there crying with blood coming out of the top of her head. Annie hugged her, putting the towel on her head.

"Sarah, stop the crying. The crying makes your head bleed more."

Amazingly, Sarah stopped the crying. Annie got the two kids in the car, grabbed her purse, and started toward the city hospital. She stopped by the gas station to tell Ken.

Ken took the towel from Sarah's head and said, "She will be all right. You won't need to take her to the hospital. It's stopped bleeding."

"I'm scared."

Ken came over and gave Annie a hug. "I'll be home in a little while. Stop worrying. Sarah will be all right."

As Ken predicted, Sarah was fine. The cut was about a quarter inch long where the swing had hit her head. Ken knew more about raising kids then she did because he was the oldest of eight children and had seen a lot.

Annie's memories had her attention and out of the corner of her eye she saw Sarah heading for the street.

Annie ran over and grabbed her. "Sarah, do you want me to get the switch after you?"

"No Mama."

"Okay, then stay away from the street."

Please Lord; keep these children safe, especially when I am alone. Protect them, she prayed as they went inside.

"Is homework all done?"

"Yes, Mama," both children said.

"Okay, you two know the routine: showers, jammies, and bed."

She had let them stay outside a little later so she needed to get them to sleep soon. She got their clothes ready for morning.

After getting them in bed she prayed, as she always did, for Ken. She got in the bed and set the alarm for 6:30 a.m. She had to get the children ready for the school bus to pick them up at 7:15 a.m. They went to a school about eight miles away.

Good night, Ken, wherever you are. Tomorrow will be two weeks since he left.

Her thoughts tormented her; she was not getting much sleep. *Desertion is grounds for divorce. What would Grandma say about divorce if she were alive?* Annie answered her thoughts. *She would say if this experience is bringing Ken closer to God, it should be worth it for you to go through rough times. I remember one day at Grandma's, Dad came to pick me up. He and Grandma were talking in the living room and I had come in the back door and overheard them. I didn't hear what Dad said to Grandma but I could hear Grandma's scolding voice.*

I heard Grandma say, "John, you have to stay with her. What would happen to those four children if you divorced her?"

The night before Mom had started a fight the same way she had many times before, yelling and hollering at him because his ride to work dropped him off late. Dad never fought back. This time she grabbed him by the throat and was choking him. Annie's two older brothers had pulled her off of him.

    Mom yelled at him every day just as soon as he got home from work. Dad was the safety net for us kids. He would try to make a joke to take away the burden from us kids. I swore when I got married that I would not yell at my husband. There were times when I would confront Ken about working too much. Maybe if I had been louder he would have listened. Annie answered herself. *No he wouldn't. Just like before he just said if we were going to argue, he would go back to work some more. He knew how I felt so I backed off as usual.*

It was 9:30 p.m. and the phone rang.

"Hello?"

She heard Becky's voice. "Sorry to call so late but I have some news that may give you the answer to the why."

"It's okay. Tell me. I don't know why he left, where he is, or anything. I thought about calling his family in Georgia but did not want them to get upset if he wasn't there."

"It has got to be hard not knowing where he is living. I am praying for your peace through all of this turmoil. I believe God answered the why today."

"What happened?"

"I saw Norma at the grocery store a little bit ago and she asked about you."

"You mean the bookkeeper where Ken worked?"

"Yes, and she had heard Ken wasn't here in town but expected he was looking for a job. She told me Ken came to her office that last Friday to get his paycheck."

"Yes, they get paid Friday mornings and then start their pay week on Friday for the next week."

"She told me he came in that Friday morning and told her he was quitting and wouldn't be back."

"Did he say why?"

"No, but later in the afternoon she found out that Larry the mechanic had been given Ken's job as parts manager and the boss put Ken back working with the mechanics. The boss told Ken he was too good a mechanic to be in parts."

"Oh my! That would have been a terrible blow to Ken. He spent weeks getting all those parts together from the old building. They were piled in boxes. He categorized them and put them in pigeon-hole-type shelving, labeling them all. I was proud of him and told him so. Parts manager was a step up for him. He must have been crushed."

"Norma said everyone at the shop felt sorry for Ken. He had really done an excellent job."

"Thank you for letting me know, Becky. This answers why he was upset, but not why he didn't tell me. He just left."

"We will keep praying and find him. Don't be discouraged."

Annie hung up the phone and crawled in the bed. *Thank you, Lord, for this much-needed information. You are an awesome God and I know you will answer my prayers for Ken. I will try to be patient.*

CHAPTER 10

ANNIE'S FAITH WAS growing. She was a practical person who searched the Bible and believed every word came straight from God. What she was going through didn't seem practical. Most women would have filed for divorce. She decided to trust God to work this situation out. She would do her best in the meantime to follow the Lord and be an example for her children.

Going to work at Dr. B.'s office kept her busy in the daytime. Dr. Beet was sensitive about his name so she called him Dr. B. He was an optometrist and this was the fifth year she worked for him. He had given her a raise every year, so now she was making five dollars an hour. That amount was plenty to support her and the children. No woman she knew made that much money. Nevertheless, she didn't waste her money. She remembered how hard it was for them to make it financially in the first years of their marriage. She made sure she gave a tithe to the church before she spent the money she earned. She started putting a small amount of money in savings each week.

Dr. B. realized how well she dealt with children and made her his assistant. Annie gave tests to the children and adults who came for glasses. Dr. B. had some great ideas to help children see.

Visual training was given to children who were cross-eyed. To test the children Dr. B. had them walk a balance beam the size of a railroad tie in the visual room. If they were cross-eyed they couldn't walk the beam. They would fall off the beam as they tried. These children would be able to walk that beam before he was through with their visual training. The training was one hour a week for three to six months. One of the machines they looked into at the training room had two balls about an inch apart, and as the patient turned the knob those two balls moved about six inches apart. When the patient turned it back, it became two inches again. Doing this repetitively exercised the eye muscles. Dr. B. said exercising the muscles of the eyes was the answer, not surgery. The muscles in the patient's eyes were being trained to stay in place. By realigning the muscles, it brought the eyes where they should be, stopping them from looking toward the middle. Annie was skeptical about the process at first and then she saw it actually worked.

Dr. B. gave Annie a book to read by Dr. Doman and Dr. Delacato. They were neurological specialists that believed neurologically damaged brains of children could be retrained through special methods. Some eye problems were being helped also. They had the children crawl on the floor like a baby. Their theory was that the brain is trained while a baby crawls on the floor. If they miss that period in their life, their brain does not develop right. They believed it could be retrained by putting them through a crawling conditioning.

The forms the parents filled in at Dr. B.'s office asked two preliminary questions. One was "Did your child crawl when a baby?" The second one, "If they crawled, how long did they crawl?" Nine out of ten children who were cross-eyed did not crawl as babies at all. The parents would brag, "Oh, Johnny was so smart he just pulled himself up to the coffee table and started walking."

Another test that was given was a paper with a big circle on it. Annie told the child to make a face out of the circle with the crayon she gave them. Annie was so surprised to see the way children drew the eyes in the circle. One who couldn't see well drew squinty eyes. Sometimes a child drew one eye in the middle of the circle. After doing a refraction test on the child who drew one eye, Dr. B. diagnosed that child with lazy eye syndrome. The children were drawing how they were seeing. Dr. B. would tell the parents of such children to wear a patch over their good eye, forcing the lazy eye to work.

Annie also gave the glaucoma test for those over forty. A big black piece of felt about four feet wide and long was hung on the wall. There was a white dot in the middle of that screen. Annie put a patch over the person's one eye and sat the patient about four feet away from the screen.

She used a black wand with a white dot on the very end to detect the dimensions of the blind spot on both sides. Starting from the middle she put the wand with the white dot next to the dot on the screen. She told the patient to keep their eye on the middle white dot and let Annie know when the white dot on the wand disappeared as she pulled the wand out to each side. She would mark these areas with pins. It would show how big the blind spot was for each eye. The doctor was able to detect different problems within the eye from abnormal blind spot patterns. The normal blind spot was about six inches in diameter.

Not only could he detect glaucoma, but the doctor also could detect other irregularities like cataracts and macular degeneration. Being an optometrist, he could not treat these patients, but he referred them to an ophthalmologist who could do surgery.

Dr. B. was a perfectionist and had all the glasses ordered from the laboratory rechecked to see if they were made correctly. Rechecking was Annie's responsibility using a lensometer. Most of the time the glasses were made correctly, but once in a while Annie found errors. Then the glasses were returned to the lab and made over again.

She filled in for the receptionist when she was out of the office. Esther was not absent very much, but since she fitted the patients with the frames to order the glasses, Annie learned to do that also. Esther was a middle-aged woman whom Dr. B. had met at a restaurant along with her husband. Dr. B. asked her to come to the office for an interview. She told him her chief qualifications were she could dust and she was bored with staying at home after her children were raised and gone. Dr. B. found her to be just the right person for the job. Annie enjoyed working with her. She was very personable and she could collect money out of people in such a way they thought she was doing them a favor. She would ask them, with a big smile on her face, "Do you want to pay your bill with check or cash?" No other alternative was available. Esther could wind Dr. B. around her little finger. It was a delight to watch. When it came to the patients and their needs, she made sure they got the best care.

Annie learned much from Dr. B. and Esther. She felt good around them. Because Dr. B. was a perfectionist, Annie had a rough time the first month or so but she caught on quick. Since he gave her a raise each year, he apparently felt her work was good although he didn't say so often. Esther had told her, "Dr. B. likes your work. He usually fires his assistant candidates after two weeks. He really got upset if they put out glasses that weren't right, or a test wasn't given to a child correctly."

Annie had a full day every day. Her mind was occupied with her work. It was the nights and weekends that were hard to get through. She spent most Saturdays cleaning the house and washing clothes. One Saturday she took the kids north a few miles and picked some Concord grapes. Annie had the children help her make jelly with them. Grape was Ken's favorite jelly as well as Kenny's.

Corn roasts were a big thing in the country. The farmers dumped a lot of freshly picked corn still in the husks in a tub of water, soaking it good, and then put them in a pile and built a huge fire over it. When the fire burned down, the corn was raked out of the coals and let to cool awhile. Then you could husk the corn and eat it. It sure was good eating it that way. Sitting around the fire eating corn on the cob with your friends and neighbors was always fun. She would have gone if Ken were there, but everyone would ask too many questions. Depending on where it was held, there might be beer to drink. Annie did not want to take the children or go herself where alcohol was served.

She checked the mail at the post office every day hoping for a letter from Ken. She had gotten a letter from her family last week. She hesitated to answer, but then decided she could talk about what the children were doing. She answered the letter so they would not call and want to know what was wrong.

Annie was very lonesome and concerned about Ken's disappearance, but she trusted the Lord would get her through this ordeal one way or another. She would hope for Ken to come back but plan as if he wasn't.

CHAPTER 11

IT HAD BEEN three full weeks since Ken left. It was the Saturday of Kenny's birthday. Annie thought, *Surely Ken will call Kenny to wish him happy birthday.* Kenny was nine years old and Annie planned a birthday party for him to take his mind off of the fact that his dad was not there. Annie invited all the neighbor kids in for a party.

They played typical birthday party games like pin the tail on the donkey. They ate sloppy joes and potato chips and drank Kool-Aid. Then Annie brought out the chocolate birthday cake she had made. All the children joined in singing "Happy Birthday." Kenny excitedly opened his presents. Annie bought him a new Bible that he seemed to appreciate. He had gotten saved at vacation Bible school (VBS) in the summer.

Annie told them they could all play in the yard until their parents came to get them. When Kenny went outside, at the side door, there was a Schwinn coaster bike with his name on the ribbon. It wasn't new—it would take a full week's pay to buy a brand-new one—but it was one Annie got for twenty dollars. The dentist, who had an office next door to Dr. B., asked her if she wanted it for Kenny. They had one they wanted to sell. Kenny got on right away and tried to balance it. This was his first two-wheeler bike.

"You will have to wait until I can help you ride it, because you have never ridden a two-wheeled bike before this. You can only ride it in the yard unless someone older is watching you on the street or the sidewalk in front of the store. The driveway here is pretty long, so that would be a good place to start."

"Thanks, Mama, I love it," Kenny said as he ran over and hugged Annie.

Autumn had snuck up on Annie and she realized it was getting dusk outside. She and her children walked all the children home that lived close by. As they got back to the house, Annie saw Becky pull up in her car to pick her two girls up. Becky came in the house and said, "I will help you clean up after the party."

"Thank you, Becky. You are a true friend."

They finished cleaning up and Becky said, "I need to get home, but let's sit down and talk a few minutes. How are you doing?"

"Becky, it is hard, especially today. I thought for sure Ken would call Kenny on his birthday."

"I would never think this of Ken. He seems like a happy-go-lucky guy without a care in the world. From what I have noticed he gets along well with people."

"He had to be really upset with his boss to quit like that without notice, but I know that his boss was taking advantage of his hard work. Knowing why he quit does not explain to me why he didn't let me know where he was going. He probably went to Decatur to his family, but if I call down there and he is not there, his family will be as worried as I am."

"I guess you are right about that. Perhaps tomorrow after church you can talk to Pastor West about the new developments. He could maybe lend a man's viewpoint. Now let me pray with you before I go."

The next morning's sermon was very uplifting, as Pastor talked about how God loves us all the time, especially when bad things come into a Christian's life. What seems bad may be for our own good.

Pastor said he would be glad to talk with Annie. They sat down in the sanctuary after everyone left. Mary took the kids in the fellowship hall and found them some Kool-Aid to drink.

"Pastor, it has been three weeks and two days since Ken left without a word. I have found out that he quit his job, which was probably justified, from what he and others he worked with daily have said. How long do I go on before I think about divorce? Desertion is a legitimate reason for divorce in the state of Michigan. Is it in the Bible?"

"I don't know Ken well. He did come over to our driveway and help me get the car started one day last month. He told me the part I needed for the car, and when I got it, he put it on for me. I know he has a good heart."

"I am glad he helped you, Pastor. He is good about doing things for people when he knows how to help."

"A man's work means a lot to him, probably as much as a woman's home and children mean to her. That does not give him reason to desert you. Is there a Biblical reason for divorce? In I Corinthians chapter seven, there are some verses that make it clear that, if a husband leaves, a wife is not under bondage. You should read that chapter today and meditate on it. It also states that your children are sanctified when only one in the marriage is saved. That just means the believer has a good chance of having influence on those children because God has set them apart for him.

"Please notice Verse 16: 'For what knowest thou, O wife, whether thou shalt save thy husband? Or how knowest thou, O man, whether thou shalt save thy wife?'

"This verse in no way means a man can have salvation by his wife. A man can only be saved by the Lord Jesus Christ, but you living your life in front of him may be the way that he does come to know the Lord.

"There is also another verse in I Peter 3:1, 'Likewise, ye wives, be in subjection to your own husbands; that, if any obey not the word, they also may without the word be won by the conversation of the wives.' That word conversation means way of life. I know it is hard for you, Annie, but if you can believe that God is working this situation out for good, I think you will find the answers you need."

"Pastor, I guess I am at the place where I can say to God, 'I believe, help my unbelief.' I know that God will take care of me and the children whether Ken comes back or not. I just want to know why he has not called us wherever he is staying."

Pastor had prayer with Annie asking God to prepare her heart, and that specifically she would hear from Ken before the next Sunday.

Pastor said to Annie after the prayer, "God is working; just because you only hear silence doesn't mean He is not there. Sometimes He wants us to listen better to our hearts. You need your heart prepared for what is to come. Right now it seems very painful but joy will come eventually. The longer I know Him the more I am sure He is working on this problem. He has shown you why Ken probably left. God is preparing your heart and He is also working on Ken. This may be a step in Ken coming closer to being saved."

"Thank you, Pastor."

Annie left the church feeling a peace.

Annie thought of the verse II Corinthians 5:17, "Therefore if any man be in Christ, he is a new creature: old things are passed away; behold all things are become new."

God is working on Ken to get him to the place where he can become a new creature. I just have to be patient.

CHAPTER 12

ANNIE SPENT TIME on her knees that night after talking to the pastor about divorce. She read and reread the Scriptures he pointed out to her. She cried out to the Lord to give her answers no matter how hard it was for her to handle. It was late when she crawled in the bed.

She woke up the next morning sobbing like she had a dream that made her cry, but she couldn't remember it. She looked at the clock. It was 7:00 a.m. She forgot to set the alarm. *The kids will miss the school bus. Oh, well, I can take them.*

She quickly woke the children.

"Hurry kids, your mama slept in and you have missed the bus. I will have to take you to school."

The kids scrambled out of their beds as Annie went to the telephone. She dialed Esther's number.

"Good morning Esther."

"Not so good morning today. It is foggy out there."

"Will you please tell Dr. B. that I will be late this morning? I forgot to set my alarm clock and the kids have missed the school bus. I am going to take them to school before I go to work."

She put some bowls on the table and several boxes of cereal along with the jug of milk. She put the coffeepot on the stove to start boiling.

"You kids, fix yourselves some cereal while I get dressed. Kenny, let me know when the water boils up in the coffeepot so I can turn the burner off."

"Yes, I will, Mama."

After she was dressed and poured herself some coffee, she quickly said the morning blessing with the kids. She grabbed the kids' lunches out of the refrigerator, thankful she had made them the night before.

"Both of you get in the back seat this morning."

"Why can't I ride in the front?" Kenny moaned.

"Esther said there is a lot of fog this morning. I want you children safe in that back seat if I have to stop suddenly. You sit still back there and be quiet so I can concentrate on my driving."

"Okay."

"Do you both have your books?"

"Yes, Mama," they said together.

She was about halfway to school when she noticed fog coming up from the river. She slowed down and turned on her lights. It got thicker as she drove on. She couldn't see anything. Following the side of the road she crept along about twenty miles an hour. Suddenly she saw lights ahead and stopped but crashed right into the back of a school bus that had stopped to pick up kids. She put on her blinker lights and said under her breath, "What next?"

"Kids, are you okay? Anyone hurt?"

"No one's hurt, Mama, we are okay, but boy are you in trouble hitting a school bus," said Kenny.

"Stay in the car."

She got her driver's license and insurance card out of her wallet and got out of the car. She could see the school bus was not hurt at all. Her front fender and the boot or trunk of the car was banged in a little. Since the boot was in the front of the '64 Volkswagen, there was no motor to worry about being damaged.

The school bus driver came back to where she was and said, "Are you all right, ma'am?"

"Yes, we are fine. What about the children on the school bus?"

"That bump wasn't hard enough to even rock the bus. They are all fine. The lady at this house called the police."

"Thank you. I am so glad no one was injured."

Annie went back to sit in the car with the kids until the police came. She barely got into the car and explained to the kids they had to wait for the police when the police car pulled up behind her. When the police had all the information and the school bus driver was ready to leave, Annie asked the bus driver, "The fog is lifting a little. Could you take my children on the bus so I can take care of reporting the accident to my insurance company?"

"I'll be glad to, Mrs. Jenkins."

"Thank you," she said to the bus driver. "Kenny and Sarah, get on the school bus; I'll see you tonight after school."

The police officer came to her car and said very kindly, "I am not going to issue a ticket for the accident, because it was just too hard to see anything this morning. I could tell you weren't going fast or the bus would have a dent in it. Give this police report to your insurance agent."

"Thank you so much, Officer. I really appreciate you for not writing a ticket."

"You are welcome; the fog is lifting so drive carefully."

Annie got in the car and drove cautiously to their insurance agency.

"Hello, Mr. Elliott. I have bad news for you."

Mr. Elliott said, "I have just got in the office and was having a cup of coffee. Would you like one?"

"I think I could use one, thanks."

Mr. Elliott was the fatherly type and easy to talk with. Annie figured his gift for gab made him a good salesman. She showed him the police report.

"I was late getting up this morning and had to take the children to school and ran into the stopped school bus over on Maysville Road."

He glanced at the report and said, "The officer did not give you a citation. That's the good news. I guess you could use some good news. Your family is having bad luck this past couple weeks?"

"What do you mean?"

"Well, with the Mustang being stolen a week ago Friday and now this accident..." He stopped talking and looked at her intently. Mr. Elliott knew something was wrong by the expression on Annie's face. "Oh, you didn't know Ken had already reported the stolen car down there in Decatur? He called me from Georgia and told me about it. The insurance paid off the loan on the car, but it won't pay for the toolbox, money, and clothes that were stolen from the back seat. Don't worry about it. The insurance will pay for both cars."

"Thank you for the coffee, Mr. Elliott; I will wait until Ken gets back to get the VW fixed."

"Okay. Tell him to let me see the estimate for the damage and I'll send the check."

"Yes, sir, and have a good day."

Annie wanted to get out of there before she broke down crying.

As she left, Mr. Elliott said, "Don't worry about the VW, Mrs. Ken. It will be all covered. You have a good day too."

She had mixed emotions about what she had just heard. The Mustang and Ken's tools and money were stolen. How did that happen? And on the other side was Pastor's prayer to find out where Ken was before next Sunday, which had come true the next day. *I guess I should be praising the Lord for answered prayer.*

Annie drove on to work, only two hours late. When she explained to Dr. B. about the accident, he was very understanding. He had gotten behind on the morning appointments because Annie wasn't there and he had to do the tests himself. Annie got right to it and they were finished with morning appointments by noon. Dr. B. took a long lunch and didn't start appointments in the afternoon until 2:00 p.m., which gave him time to catch up if he got behind.

Esther said he took naps on that long lunch. He always went home. Annie didn't believe Esther at first and she told Annie to look at the chenille bedspread pattern on the side of his face when he comes back. Annie saw it one day and figured Esther was right as usual. Once a month he would invite Esther and Annie to lunch at his house. His wife always made a good lunch. Annie noticed when they had been there thirty minutes or so Dr. B. would look at his watch.

Esther said later, "We were messing up his naptime."

As she was leaving that night, she saw Dr. Mark, the dentist, in the hall and said, "Kenny was so happy to get that bike. Thank you so much for bringing it out to the apartment for me and tying that pretty ribbon on it."

"Glad to do it for a pretty young lady like yourself. The ribbon was my wife's doing."

"You thank her for me, please."

"I will. Have a good night."

"Thank you. I hope you do too."

As Annie drove home she couldn't wait until she could get on the phone and call Ken in Decatur, Georgia.

CHAPTER 13

AS SHE DIALED the Jenkins' number in Decatur she prayed, *Oh Lord, help me to talk to Ken without anger in my voice.*

A younger voice answered, "Hello, Jenkins residence."

"Hello, Ronnie, this is your favorite sister-in-law. How are you doing?"

"I'm fine, and you are my only sister-in-law. Did you hear about Ken's Mustang? He let Dad take me to school a couple times in it before it was stolen."

"Yes; I heard about Ken's Mustang. Is he there so I could talk to him?"

"No, Michael took him to ride around town and see if they could spot the Mustang. They have been doing that every night when they get off work."

"Are both of them working for your dad?"

"Yes, they are tearing down an old apartment building."

"Will you tell Ken I called and asked for him to call me back collect?"

"I will. Dad doesn't like those long-distance charges on his telephone bill."

"Yes, Ronnie, I know, that is why I want you to remind Ken to call collect."

"Okay, I'll write him a message in case I am asleep when they come back."

Annie thought when she hung up the phone, *Well, it didn't seem like a surprise to Ronnie that I called Ken there. Ken's family doesn't know he left me that note and rode off with no explanation. They have no idea that I have been here scared, worried, and crying my heart out because I have not heard from him for three and a half weeks. He must be acting like this is a visit. He doesn't plan to stay or Ronnie would have asked more questions.*

When Ken had gotten out of the service, they moved to Georgia. Ken bought an old tandem dump truck to haul dirt and worked for his dad filling in old lots. He had the truck two months and blew up the motor in it. The story of his life: motors blowing up because of his heavy foot. Trouble with truck motors: they cost lots of money to replace. He still had to make payments on the truck. He sold the truck to a company that had the money to fix it and got out of making the payments.

That left him making minimum wage working for his dad. Annie adapted as she always did and went to work at a Howard Johnson's restaurant to supplement their income. They continued living in the basement apartment at the family home. They stayed in Decatur about six months. Ken came to Annie one day and said, "We are moving back to Michigan."

Annie said, "When do we leave? I would like to give my boss a week's notice."

"I called Randy; he is putting in swimming pools now. I can work for him right away. There is an empty apartment downstairs from where we used to live. We will leave as soon as you get ready."

Annie called her boss and just told her, "I have to quit. We are moving." They were packed up and ready to go in two days.

They moved back to Michigan and it really felt like home to both of them. Sometimes Annie would see a faraway look in Ken's eyes. She wondered if he was longing to go back to Georgia. Every year they took their vacation and went there. Ken would always work for his dad the whole time. Annie would work around the house helping with cooking and cleaning.

She could not understand the draw to his family, especially since his cousin had told her how abusive his dad was to Ken. His cousin had observed Ken's dad using a two-by-four over his back because he wasn't working hard enough. He was only twelve years old, carrying big cement blocks up a ladder to workmen building a gas station. Yet Ken seemed strangely drawn to this family. She figured he must have gone there this time because he wanted to show off the Mustang to them.

Ken never told her any of those rough stories; he was fiercely loyal to his family. The only thing he ever talked about was running away from home three times. *Well, he did it again. He ran away from here, but he will not do that again, not as my husband.*

She had just put the kids in bed when the phone rang.

The operator said, "Collect call from Ken Jenkins. Will you accept the charges?"

"I'll accept the call, Operator."

"Go ahead," Annie heard her say to Ken.

"Hello, this is Ken."

"I still recognize your voice; it hasn't been that long that I have forgotten the sound. Matter of fact, it still gives me butterflies."

"Oh, unreal!" Ken replied. Ken always said unreal when Annie complimented him on his good looks or how he made her feel.

"Well, I guess you want to know why I called," she said.

"It is good to hear your voice, Annie."

"I finally found out where you were after over three weeks of worrying, crying myself to sleep, and being scared to death you had been in an accident somewhere and died and no one knew who you were or maybe you had run off with another woman. I found out today from Mr. Elliott where you were; up to then, it was anyone's guess."

"Oh, he told you about the Mustang."

"Yes, I asked Pastor West to pray with me that we would find you. Just yesterday he prayed that we would know before another week had gone by where you were. I had to get into an accident to find out, but God does answer prayers."

"What happened? Was anyone hurt?"

"It was extremely foggy and I got up late and had to take the kids to school. I ran into the back of the stopped school bus on Maysville Road. The bus was hardly touched, but the boot of the VW is bent in and so is the fender. You usually take care of those things, but you weren't here so I stopped to show Mr. Elliott the police report. He said he was sorry we were having so many problems. I looked at him dumbfounded. He told me about the Mustang getting stolen in Decatur. Until today,

I had no idea where you were staying, if you had another woman you were living with, or what you were up to; because all I got was a note which said, 'I can't stand it anymore. I have to leave.' Now can you add anything to those nine words?"

Annie continued. "But before we discuss the divorce, I would like you to talk to Kenny and Sarah. I have put them to bed, but they need to hear from their father. You do remember this past Saturday was Kenny's birthday?" She didn't wait for an answer. "Kenny, Sarah," she called, "Daddy is on the phone."

Annie tried to quiet down her heart after giving that big description of her feelings to Ken. She could hear Kenny say, "Hello, Daddy, we miss you." A pause and then, "Thank you, Daddy. Mama had a birthday party for me and I got a new Schwinn bike." Another pause and "Mama helped me get balanced at first but I am riding it up and down the driveway by myself. It is so neat."

Sarah said, "My turn Kenny," Sarah grabbed the phone and said, "Hello Daddy. Did you know Mama ran into the school bus?" A pause. "We weren't hurt. We made you some grape jelly. We picked the grapes, and Mama let me help make the jelly. When will you be home?" Pause. "I miss you too, Daddy."

"Okay, kids, get back in your beds. I need to talk to Daddy now. Are you ready to answer some questions now, Ken?"

"I just assumed you knew where I went. I didn't tell you I was going because I knew you would talk me out of it. The feelings on the note had nothing to do with you. I was upset about being demoted at work. I couldn't face you or anyone else. I was on my way back home to Michigan two Fridays ago. It was a bit chilly so I left the Mustang running while I went into an all-night Krystal and got some hamburgers to take with me. I came out and the car, my toolbox, and my suitcase were gone. I had put the money I made working for Dad that week in the suitcase. I just had my wallet with me. Michael has been riding me all over Decatur looking for that Mustang for two weeks. Just tonight the police called and said they found it totaled, south of here almost in Florida. Toolbox, clothes, and money were gone. Now, what did I leave out?"

"How long have we been married?" Annie said calmly.

"It will be ten years next month."

"In any one of those days we have been married, have I ever been able to stop you from doing something you wanted to do?"

"No, but I knew if I saw you that just looking in those beautiful green eyes would have stopped me. I really don't know why you didn't call and see if I was here."

"What would I have told your parents if you weren't there? Should I have read the note to them and gotten them worried also?" Annie replied. "Now, tell me why it has not occurred to you that I would be worried, after all these days, going on the fourth week? What about your son's birthday?"

"Time just got away from me. I planned to come home that Friday and the car was stolen. I have been worried sick about that thing. I forgot it was Kenny's birthday. I have been working with my dad to get some money to get home."

"Is that what you are going to tell the divorce judge when I file for divorce because of desertion? 'I had this problem so I ran home to Mama and Daddy to let them solve it for me. My car was stolen. I just forgot to call my wife and kids for twenty-three days. Yes, Your Honor, I am thirty years old.'"

"No, Annie, I hope you get that word divorce out of your mind. I love you and the kids. I just wasn't thinking straight. Please forgive me." Annie heard his voice break.

"I am angry right now; I am going to pray about what to do. Pastor West says divorce is not the answer, even though I have grounds for it. Whenever you decide if, when, and how you plan to come home to us, call me collect and we will talk again."

Annie hung up the phone and stepped outside so the kids couldn't hear what she was doing. She laughed and laughed. *I am going to let him squirm and learn a lesson. I am tired of being taken for granted.*

Annie slept well that night.

CHAPTER 14

TUESDAY AFTERNOON ANNIE got home from work at five-thirty and went to get the kids at Mrs. Anderson. As they came in the apartment door she heard the phone ringing. She picked it up and said, "Hello."

The operator said, "A collect call from Ken Jenkins. Will you accept the charges?"

"Yes, Operator, I will accept the charges. Hello, Ken. You called so soon."

"Annie, I have thought through all that I have done. I have acted like a fool. I am sorry for all the pain and hurt I caused you. I wanted to make sure you knew as soon as possible I do want to come home. Please forgive me."

"Ken, when I married you I took you for better or worse. I promised to love, honor, and obey. I haven't changed my mind. Somehow God has given to me a great love for you. I am looking forward to having you home. I just want you to know that you need not come home if you don't plan to be my husband and father to our children. I do completely forgive you, and it will not be mentioned again."

"Thank you, Annie, for saying all that. I don't deserve you, but I will be the best husband and father I know how to be. I have to work this week with Dad so I will have some money to buy the ticket to come home. There is a Greyhound bus that leaves at ten out of Decatur Friday night. It arrives in Detroit at eleven Saturday morning. Will you be able

THE MAKING OF A NEW CREATURE

to pick me up? If you can't, I can get a local bus on to our house, but it doesn't leave Detroit until eight at night."

"I'll be there at eleven and I am very anxious to see you. I love you, Ken."

"I'll see you then. Bye."

Annie knew she, as a Christian, had to forgive, but the overwhelming love she had for Ken made it very easy. She called the pastor and then Becky to tell them where Ken was and that he would be home Saturday. She asked Pastor and Mary if they would watch the kids Saturday morning while she went to get Ken. They were glad to help. Pastor rejoiced that our prayers were answered, even though it caused a car accident.

The kids were excited all week to know Daddy would be home and now the day was here. Annie decided to leave by nine. It would be a good hour-and-a-half drive and she wasn't sure she knew the way very well. The bus station was at Cadillac Square east of Woodward, right in downtown Detroit. She had been to downtown Detroit with Becky a couple of times Christmas shopping at Hudson's. Hudson's was a thirty-two-story building with twenty-five stories of shopping and was a city block wide and long. She knew you couldn't miss that store. She had seen the bus station when they were there shopping, so she had a pretty good idea where she needed to go. Becky also gave her some good instructions.

She dropped the kids off at the West house earlier and was well on her way. The pastor told the kids they were going for a hike in the woods behind their house to have a wiener roast. They were excited about going on a picnic with Theresa and Charlie.

She pulled in the parking lot of the bus station right on time. She got out of the car. Ken was standing at the front door and walked over to her. He had such a forlorn look on his face as he got closer to her that she put her arms out to show how welcome he was. He started smiling and took her in his arms, picking her up and swinging her around. He then kissed her long and passionately.

"Oh, how I missed my beautiful redhead," he said, putting his face and nose in her hair. "Your hair smells so good. Four weeks is a long time. I learned my lesson."

"I love you, honey," Annie said as he kissed her again.

Ken held Annie's hand as they walked to the car. "The damage on the car doesn't look too bad. Randy will let me fix it at the gas station. We can save some money that way."

Ken got in the seat to drive and Annie in the passenger side. She said, "It drives well. Would you like to stop at Kay's Kitchen for lunch?"

"Annie, I know you like to eat there. So do I, and we are close to it, but I really don't want to sit down and eat. I am anxious to get home, but I am hungry. Mama packed a sandwich and apple for me that I ate as soon as I got on the bus twelve hours ago. I fell asleep most of the way. I woke up and started worrying about how you would react when I got here. I was really scared. I am so glad you held your arms out to me. I knew then you meant it when you said you forgave me. Would you mind just stopping at a fast food drive-through so we can eat as we go home?"

"Whatever you want to do, Ken, is all right with me."

"I am such a lucky man to have found you, honey."

"Ken, there are presents for the kids in the back seat that you can give them so they know you missed them also. There is a box with an Aurora car racing set with four cars. I had it on layaway a long time for Kenny's birthday. It cost forty dollars. I saved it so you could give it to him. I also got a Raggedy Ann doll for Sarah. She will like it."

"Where did you get all the money for these gifts and a seventy-dollar Schwinn bike?"

Annie explained it was a used bike and how she gave Dr. Mark five dollars a week until he had twenty. The car set was on layaway before Ken had left.

Ken pulled in the driveway and hopped out of the car and went in the house with Annie. She set her purse down and said, "I'll get the kids."

"Not yet. I want to know if you missed me as much as I missed you."

He took her in his arms and kissed her over and over and picked her up and carried her into the bedroom. Kicking the door shut, he sat her down on the bed. "I won't ever leave you again; I do not ever want to lose you."

Later, Annie got the kids and watched as they greeted their father with lots of hugs. Ken gave them the presents. Sarah loved her doll and Kenny was ecstatic to get the race car set.

Annie fixed Ken meatloaf for supper, one of his favorite meals. As she was cleaning up the kitchen after supper, she glanced over the kitchen counter and saw Kenny and Ken playing with the race car set on the living room floor. Her heart was so full of love; she got a camera and took a picture of them playing on the floor.

"I hate to break this up, guys, but it is time for showers and bed."

"Okay, Mama. We sure are having fun."

"I know, Kenny, and you both can play again. If you scoot that track out of the middle of the floor, you can leave it up."

Ken had gotten a shower earlier while Annie had gone to get the kids at Wests house. Annie had bought some underwear, socks, and one set of clothes for Ken earlier in the week. He had taken almost everything with him and had gotten it stolen.

"Kenny and Sarah are ready for bed," Annie said. "Ken, will you tuck the kids in, and be sure to listen to their prayers, while I get my shower?"

"Sure honey."

After her shower Annie went in the bedroom where Ken had already climbed in the bed.

"Annie, did you know the kids pray for me to get saved?"

"Yes, every night, as I do also. The most important thing that can happen to a person is to come to know the Lord Jesus Christ. Would you go to church with us tomorrow?"

"No, I have to take your car and see if I can get it fixed and find me transportation to go to a new job."

"What new job?"

"I called Walter, my former military friend. He lives close by and said if I get a job at the car factory in Pontiac I can ride with him. He said they are hiring. He is retiring in a couple months but that will give me opportunity to find a car if I get the job."

"You would go right by Dr. B.'s office to go to Pontiac, so you can take me to work Monday and pick me up at five o'clock after you have gone to Pontiac to apply for a job."

That night Annie slept with her husband close to her. Whatever his problems were, for now, it was good. He wanted her to lie in his arms while he slept. Annie knew she could lie there until he went to sleep. Pretty soon his arm would start jerking from the pressure of her head on his arm. That happened every time Ken wanted Annie to sleep in his arms. She would move over so he could sleep peacefully. His worries were gone now. She had to keep praying until he got saved. God does answer prayers. He had proved that to her once more.

CHAPTER 15

KEN GOT A job with a construction company building houses. Jake also worked there with him. Jake and Ken got along very well together. Jake's father was very abusive to him, so they had that in common. Ken sympathized with him; he also was a very good worker. It would only last a couple months until winter arrived. Ken had been told at the car factory they would be hiring in a couple months. Walter would not be working then so he had to find his own way to work.

Ken's boss had invited him to a men's retreat at Camp Barakel. Several men from Annie's church were going, including Pastor West. Much to Annie's surprise, Ken went. It started on Friday evening and lasted through Sunday morning's chapel service.

Annie kept praying Ken would realize he was a lost sinner and needed to be saved. When she and the children got home from church Sunday, Ken had just pulled in the driveway. She had a roast in the oven and only had to put the carrots in and cook the potatoes to mash. While the food finished cooking, Annie sat next to Ken on the couch and said, "Tell me all about the camp. You look relaxed."

"I guess I did get rested up; those bunk beds weren't too bad. I shared a bunk with Phillip Bassett, who turned out to be what I would call a real Christian. He goes to that little church in Canfield. He is younger than me and seemed genuine. He has only been married two years."

"What does 'a real Christian' mean?"

"A real Christian does not go to church on Sunday and the bars on

Saturday night. I have drank beer at the bar with some of the men at your church.

"Oh, I didn't know that," Annie said with surprise in her voice.

Ken went on, "Phillip wasn't preachy; he just knew what he believed and didn't mind telling those who asked."

"How were the speakers?"

"Okay, I guess. I liked hearing Mr. Maxwell; he told of his love for people and for the Lord. He gives a good portion of his income back to the Lord."

"Where does he work?"

"He owns the Sveden House restaurants, spelled with a v and he pronounces the v. They are smorgasbord-type restaurants, with all-you-can-eat food bars. Very family oriented. His first one was in Lansing but they have one close to Pontiac now in Utica. I'd like to go sometime."

"Let's go Friday or Saturday?"

"Okay, that sounds good; I got a card with the address of the restaurant on it. Speaking of food, is dinner about ready?" Ken said, giving Annie a kiss.

Annie jumped up. "Give me ten minutes."

Friday night Ken picked Annie up at work; she changed her clothes at the office and hurried to the car. Her work was halfway to Pontiac. It saved time for her not to go home. The kids were excited to be going out to a restaurant with Mama and Daddy.

As they walked in the Sveden House they saw an unbelievable number of counters of food; one for meat, one for salads, one for vegetables, one for desserts with an ice cream dispenser. They had never seen anything like it. Next to the meat counter was a table where a man was cutting roast beef continually, serving it to each person who asked for it.

The restaurant was clean. Waitresses and cashiers had Swedish dresses and bonnets. Annie realized she needed to give some instructions.

"Kenny and Sarah, you may eat as much as you want, but don't take a lot of one thing because you may not like it. You do not get a dessert plate until you eat your regular food. You may get a glass of soda pop at the dispenser but do not get a second one without showing me your plate. Now we will say the blessing. You can get a plate and go get what you want after we pray. You come right back to this table."

Kenny said the blessing and then took off with Sarah behind him. Annie tried small portions of the fried chicken, Swedish meatballs, and halibut. They had fried shrimp but Annie was allergic to shellfish so she didn't try it. Bread pudding was a specialty of the house so Annie tried that as well. What she liked even better was their glorified rice with marshmallows and cherries. It was better than any Annie had ever eaten. The waiters and waitresses were all so polite and kind to everyone.

Ken said, "Do you all want to go back for seconds?"

Kenny said, "I want some more ice cream?"

"Okay," Annie said, "but just a half cup this time."

"Yes, Mama."

Annie looked at Ken and said, "Thanks for bringing us here. The kids will talk about this for a long time, and so will I. The salad bar was out of this world. This is the first time I ate carrot-and-raisin salad. The macaroni salad was delicious."

"I don't care anything about salads, but the mashed potatoes, roast beef, and gravy were really great," Ken said. "The chocolate cake with the sauce poured over it was really delicious."

On the way home the kids fell asleep and Annie and Ken held hands.

Annie said, "I was thinking about last year when Randy took us to the Drawbridge Inn in Canada for our tenth anniversary. That was a nice restaurant, but I really enjoyed this more. It embarrassed me when Randy ordered champagne. I was so proud of you when you spoke up and said, 'We just want ginger ale.' I was surprised at his wife, Dorothy, drinking the champagne. She goes to my church."

"Randy talked me into that restaurant because he found out it was our anniversary and asked me what I was giving you for a present. I told him I never buy you a gift; we usually just go eat at the burger place. So he sent me to the jewelry store to get you a present and made reservations for the four of us at the Drawbridge Inn."

"It was a beautiful necklace."

"I thought the green jade would go with your beautiful green eyes."

Annie leaned over and kissed Ken on the cheek. "Are you trying to get something out of me by all this flattery?"

"Is it working?"

"Probably."

Ken squeezed her hand and smiled.

CHAPTER 16

ANNIE, BECKY, AND Mary had become close through praying together and visiting people who were prospects for the church. They visited on Saturdays when Annie wasn't working and the husbands took turns babysitting. Pastor had been teaching how to lead someone to the Lord and they had marked their Bibles. Annie read and reread her notes on soul winning until she had the Romans Road to Salvation memorized. It was called the Romans Road because one verse led to another until all the steps had been read on how to show someone to salvation. After a lot of knocking on doors they finally found someone who wanted to know the plan of salvation. They led her to the Lord that evening and all three of them were praising the Lord in the car going home. What a thrill to see a person be born again into a new creature.

Annie spoke to the ladies. "I wish I could see Ken receive the Lord."

"We will all pray to that end," they both said.

Annie did not know what she would do without these dear friends.

There was a revival at the church the following week. A widow named Mrs. Cook, who lived across from the church, walked down to Ken and Annie's apartment one Friday. She mentioned that Ken had helped her with her car one day last week and she would like to invite Ken and Annie for lunch the next day. Ken said he would go, so Annie asked Mary if she and Pastor would take the kids for lunch. They agreed gladly.

Mrs. Cook had a tuna casserole that Ken did not like at all. He sat there and ate it though. Annie was quite surprised. Ken did not want to hurt Mrs. Cook's feelings.

When they were ready to leave, Annie said, "Thank you, Mrs. Cook, for that delicious meal. It is always nice not to have to cook."

Mrs. Cook said, "You are welcome, my dear. Ken, it sure would please me if you would come to the revival and sit with me this week."

Ken said, "How can I refuse such a sweet lady? I'll come on Friday night."

When they went Friday night, they sat with Mrs. Cook. The evangelist was very lively and Annie had seen many children get saved that week. Now Annie was praying for her Ken once more to trust Christ. The evangelist's scripture was Colossians 1:27, "Christ in you, the hope of Glory." He presented the gospel message very well and Annie kept hoping Ken would answer the altar call, but he didn't. He spoke to the evangelist after the meeting and found that he would be in a city about twenty-five miles away the next week.

"I want to go hear him again," Ken told Annie. "Do you want to go next Friday to that revival he will be at?"

"Yes, we can all go on Friday night."

Much to Ken's dismay, the evangelist preached the same sermon as he heard the previous Friday night. Although this discouraged Ken from going to church, Annie was encouraged that Ken was hearing the gospel message over and over. He did not realize the Lord was working on his heart.

The next Saturday they had finished a late breakfast when a knock came at the front door.

"Ken, finish your coffee. I will get the front door."

She opened the door to see two elders from the false church that Ken's family attended. The elders found them wherever they moved. Ken's mother must have given them their address each time. Ken would run out the back door when they came. He couldn't be seen in the kitchen and he just sat there this time. As a teenager Annie had heard her pastor teach on the false cults and knew how to handle herself pretty well with these elders. She had encountered visiting elders before many times.

As the elders talked to Annie about their church and beliefs, Annie let them go on talking. She finally said, "My husband is not the least bit interested in your church. He always hides when someone from your church comes here. I am a born-again Christian and believe in the grace of God, not the works you try to teach. I have Jesus in my heart and he guides me. Now let me ask you two a question. If you died today, are you 100 percent sure you would go to Heaven?"

The older of the two men said, "Well, no one can know what heaven they will progress to."

"Well, I know that I am as sure for Heaven as if I were already there. I will be there when I die. Not because of my church attendance every time the doors are open, my teaching Sunday school, singing in the choir, giving my tithe, and giving to missions, but because I know I'm a sinner and have asked Jesus Christ to forgive me of those sins. He did and shows his love to me every day. Tell me, sir, when you die and are at judgment, what are you going to tell Jesus about your sin?"

"Mrs. Jenkins, I will remind God of all the work I have done on earth and how I lived a good life."

Annie had her shorts on, which she wore on days she wasn't going anywhere, and she could see him ogling her. Annie asked, "How much work do you have to do to make up for your sin?"

He started stuttering. "I... I... I don't know."

"Well now, you want me to believe in a religion where you don't have a remedy for sin? I have the blood of Jesus covering my sins. As Jesus said in the Sermon on the Mount, the thoughts of your heart are sin also. What can you do to take care of them?"

The men stood up and the oldest one said, "I am sure you will make it to a higher heaven than I, Mrs. Jenkins. We must be on our way."

"Thank you for stopping by, men. Here's a tract for you that explains how to get rid of your sin and get to Heaven. I hope you will read it."

After she shut the door, Annie heard loud clapping in the kitchen.

"You gave them a rough time," Ken laughed.

"No, I just told them the truth."

Once again Ken heard the first part of the Gospel message that he had to do something with his sin.

"It is your family's church. You should talk to the elders," Annie said.

"It might be my family's church but it is not mine. I told you that from the time I met you. Remember I told you how my mom made me get baptized when I was twelve years old and it took three elders to put me under the water? I tried my best to get away. I have not been to that church since I ran away from home several years before I met you. I won't be going again."

Annie said, "Will you go to church with me tomorrow?"

"No, I have a football game to watch."

"The football game doesn't start until after church."

"They talk about the players and the past games before the game."

Annie gave up. "I love you anyways, Ken Jenkins," giving him a big kiss.

CHAPTER 17

WITH THE SLOWDOWN in construction and winter coming up, Ken started looking for other work. He called the automobile factory where he had applied for work a couple months ago and they told him to come in the following week. His shift would be four to midnight.

"I am glad you found work, but I sure don't like that shift. Driving fifty miles to work will mean you won't be home until after one, and you will be sleeping when I get up to get the kids ready for school and go to work myself," Annie said quietly so the kids wouldn't hear.

"Maybe after I am there awhile, I can get a dayshift. At least it's not midnight to eight in the morning. I will be making four times what I have been making."

"I have been offered a job as a bookkeeper for the same pay as Dr. B. is paying me in Maysville at a manufacturing company that makes hospital equipment."

"Well, that certainly is a lot less miles for you to drive."

"You don't mind my quitting and taking the bookkeeping job?"

"Annie, anything you do is all right with me. I trust your judgment."

"I hate leaving Dr. B. and Esther after five years. They are like family, and I love helping children, but it is more important for me to spend more time at home, especially with you working those awful hours."

"It will be okay, Annie. Come here." Ken pulled her down on his knee and gave her a kiss.

Ken rode to work with Walter for two weeks, and then Walter retired. Ken came home that Saturday with a '67 red Ford Galaxy coupe.

Annie went outside to look at the car. "This must have cost a lot."

"It is one year old and has low mileage. I can afford the payments now. I am going to start picking up three guys along the way who work in the same area I do. They will help pay for gas back and forth. Right now, I want to take my best gal for a ride. You noticed I picked out a red car for my redhead."

"If I am your best gal, who is second best?"

"Sarah, of course," Ken said, smiling. "Kenny, Sarah, let's all go for a ride."

Ken had gotten a job inspecting crankshafts at the factory. He told Annie he had to lift them off the line when a bad one came through and put it on the reject belt. He was quite bored with it.

One night when the crankshaft line stopped, he went to the assembly line and did the work for three people while the workers took a break. The union representative caught him doing it. He told Ken to never do that again. Ken told Annie he avoided the union rep for a good while. He had not joined the union and did not want to belong. He would not be able to avoid him for long though. Raised in the South, Ken was not familiar with unions and didn't want anything to do with them.

When Ken came home from work each night, he tried to be quiet, but Annie usually woke when he got in the bed. One Friday night after he had been working a couple months, Annie decided to wait for him because she could sleep in on Saturdays.

She got her Sunday school lesson out and started studying. She was teaching junior children now and loved their enthusiasm. She was always trying to think of something they could do to express their faith. Fifth and sixth graders need to get lots of Bible to get themselves spiritually ready for those teenage years.

Annie looked at the clock; it was two in the morning. She began to worry. It had snowed; did he have a wreck? She started praying. *Lord protect Ken and bring him home safe.* She got up and made a pot of coffee. She never drank coffee late at night, but she needed to stay awake in case a police officer came to tell her the bad news.

About three Annie heard a car pull in the driveway. She peeked out the curtain and saw that it was Ken.

He came in the door and said, "What are you doing up so late?"

"I decided to wait up for you since it was Friday night. More important, why are you getting home at three o'clock instead of one o'clock? With all the snow on the roads I have been terribly worried."

"Friday is payday and all my riders want to stop at this bar that cashes checks. It's the only place open, and of course they want to eat a burger and have a couple beers. Before you fuss at me, I don't drink. I am the designated driver."

"Don't you think you will be tempted to drink with them if you are in the bar?"

"Annie, I haven't drunk any alcoholic beverages in two years or better. I learned my lesson; I don't want to become a drunken bum."

Annie noticed after that night, it wasn't just Friday night Ken was late. It was often two in the morning when he came to bed. One Saturday, she sat next to him on the couch and said, "Ken, will you please do something for me?"

"If I can, I would do anything for you."

"I want you to tell your riders you are not going to stop at the bar anymore. If they want to get a ride with someone else, it's okay with you, because you want to spend more time with your wife."

"But Annie, how will I get my check cashed?"

"You could go to the bank on Saturday and put it in our account; after all, you would do anything for me."

"You trapped me."

Annie kissed him and said, "It is a nice trap though, isn't it?"

Annie worked about six months and the company laid her off because they were closing a part of the company. She talked to Ken and he told her not to worry, because he made enough money now. She could just collect her pennies from the unemployment office.

Annie had been secretly putting money in a savings account. If you deposited twenty-five dollars at a time, they gave you a free fork, knife, or spoon. Annie had accumulated eight place settings of stainless-steel ware. Ken never asked about them, so she never told him she got them for putting money in a savings account. Ken was not a good money manager, so he left the paying of the bills to Annie. He cashed his check, keeping spending money for the week, and gave Annie the rest for bills.

Being laid off gave Annie more time to spend with Becky and Mary. They would sometimes take the kids' bikes and go for rides. They spent time in prayer together once a week and went out visiting people trying to present the gospel message.

She continually prayed for Ken's salvation. Pastor West had preached a sermon about getting yourself in a condition for God to hear your prayers. He pointed out that, if there were sin in our lives, God could not hear our prayers. Annie prayed that God would show her what sin she might not have confessed. She became burdened because when Ken was home she would smoke a cigarette with him. The Bible reminded her that our bodies are the temple of God and we should not harm our bodies. She told Ken no more cigarettes; don't leave any at home for her. She found herself looking in ashtrays for cigarette butts that Ken had left around the house. She realized that even though she smoked only two or three cigarettes a day, she still was addicted to them. One day she said, "This is silly; I am down to smoking one cigarette a day and I am letting Satan control me with one lousy cigarette." That ended the desire to smoke, and she felt a burden lifted.

Ken told her that cigarettes cost only thirty-five cents a pack and not to worry about it. Annie tried to explain that it was not about the money but the control the cigarette had on her body. Ken didn't understand. She thanked the Lord for showing her the evil of them for her body.

She continued to pray that Ken would receive Christ one day soon.

CHAPTER 18

ONE NIGHT, ABOUT a month after Annie's talk with Ken about driving by himself so he wouldn't have to stop at bars, Annie heard a car pull in the driveway. She had just taken her shower and had her nightgown on with her bathrobe. She was sitting on the couch reading her Bible. It was around ten, much too early for Ken to be home.

Ken came in the house and sat on the floor at Annie's feet.

"Ken, are you sick?"

"No, I just hate myself. I feel so guilty."

"Did you quit your job?"

"No, Hilda gave me a startling statement tonight."

"Who is Hilda?"

"She is one of the supervisors on my line. She is probably in her early forties, nice looking. We sometimes eat lunch together. We talk about our families; she has a husband and three kids. She is easy to talk to because she is a good listener. Annie, if you want me to leave when I am through talking, I will. Just say so. But I want to finish talking. I have been holding this in too long. I told Hilda something about a burden I have been carrying, and she was offended."

Annie slipped down to the floor next to Ken so she could look in his eyes. Annie was fighting back the tears.

"Hilda told me I needed to go home and ask my wife to forgive me for talking to someone else about personal matters that should only be shared with a spouse. She said such personal matters usually turned into something more than just workers talking. She told me she was

79

a Christian and she would not think about breaking the vows of her marriage.

"I don't know why I did that except I just needed to talk to someone. I checked out early and drove home to talk to you. I have something that has bothered me for four years and I have to get this guilt off of me. I am a sorry husband, and you don't deserve me after what I have done. I tried drinking to forget, until the night I got drunk and was violently sick. I tried playing cards to get my mind off it. When I was around you, the guilt got worse, so I worked late night after night to keep from the guilt. When I went to Decatur, it wasn't just because of the job. I was running from the guilt, thinking that if I wasn't around you I wouldn't feel it. My car was stolen and that made me frantic looking for it, hoping I would find it. I missed you more than ever. The pain of being away from you was worse than the pain of being at home with you."

Ken continued. "I have been friendly with Hilda, and I guess it was flirting. The guilt gets worse. Driving home tonight, I knew I could not go on with my guilt. It nagged me all the way home. I beg you to forgive me." He told Annie of something that he had done about four years ago, one night of making a horrible mistake that was unthinkable and definitely hurt their marriage. "Is there any chance that you would forgive me?"

Annie could see that Ken was hurting; he had poured his soul out to her. She thanked God that Hilda, the woman he had talked with, was a Christian and put him straight. As bad as he looked, he finally looked up at Annie with tears in his eyes. "Will you forgive me?"

What he didn't know was Annie had suspected something like this and lived in dread of the day she would find out. She was not ready for it. Ken had never hit her in all their eleven years of marriage. He had always been kind to her, even when he was angry about something. She felt like he had taken his fist and punched her in the belly as hard as he could. She was in shock.

Annie couldn't talk right then. She all of a sudden felt like she had to go to the bathroom. She said as much and got up off the floor and ran to the bathroom.

She ran into the bathroom, threw off her robe, and sat on the toilet. Her whole belly was rumbling. She sat and sat and it felt like her insides were pouring out of her. She was in shock. She flushed the toilet and got in the shower again. She let the hot water pour over her as though it could take the hurt and pain away. She turned it off and dried herself, put her nightgown back on, and sat down on the toilet seat to pray. *God give me your peace and calmness as I answer Ken. Please speak through me.*

When she went out to the living room, Ken was still sitting on the floor with his head buried in his arms. She touched his arm and he jumped. "Ken, come sit on the couch next to me," she said calmly.

He got up and sat next to her. She saw tears still in his eyes.

"Ken, when we were married, I promised before God that I would love, honor, and obey you until death do us part. Have I kept that vow?"

"Yes, you have Annie; there couldn't be a more perfect wife. I am just such a sorry husband that I don't deserve you. I am willing to leave if you want me to go."

Annie continued. "You promised to love, honor, and cherish me before God until death do us part. I took my vows seriously. You have broken those vows. The Bible allows divorce in such a case, but I can see that you are genuinely repentant of those sins. God has forgiven me of my sins; how can I refuse to do the same for you?

"Do you think I haven't been tempted to break my marriage vows? Do you remember when we lived in Georgia and I worked at Howard Johnson's? A man came in every day and ordered a nickel cup of coffee and left me a dollar tip. After two or three times, he propositioned me to go to his apartment. He said he would put me up there. He said I was too pretty to have to work as a waitress. He would provide for me. His wife lived out of town. What did I do? I told him no and told you to come in the next day for coffee the same time he always came. I gave you a big hug and kiss in front of him, letting him know my husband would take care of him if he persisted."

"I never knew why you did that. I wondered."

"There were other men where I worked, but I did not give in because I remembered my vows. I ignored them and spent my breaks with women. You should be spending your breaks with men. You are just asking for trouble by spending time with women, especially pretty women who are good listeners. While you took the Mustang to Georgia and I was here alone, one night Jake came and knocked at the door. I still had my clothes on so I answered the door. Jake said he wanted to see if I needed anything. He said he knew I must be lonely. I did not let him in the house. I told him I didn't need anything, and that the kids were good company so I didn't get lonely. Besides, you were coming home at the end of the week. I hardly know Jake except to know the two of you work on cars together. I don't think I have ever said more than two words to him. What do you think he wanted?"

"He was probably testing the waters."

"Why is it that I can resist sexual advances and you feel like you can't? You don't have Christ in your heart to guide you is all I can think. Do you remember the evangelist who preached the sermon 'Christ in You, the Hope of Glory'? You liked him so well we went to hear him again at another church and he preached the same sermon at the other church?"

Ken said, "Yes, I remember."

"Well, the reason you can't resist the temptation to sin is you don't have Christ in you. When a person has Christ in the form of the Holy Spirit, He helps you fight off the temptations to be unfaithful. Ken, you have definitely hurt me with your sin more than you will ever know, but you have hurt God more. It is Jesus Christ who died on the cross for your sins that you have sinned against. Your marriage vows were made in church in the presence of God. He is who you need to ask for forgiveness. The burden you have is from God. As long as we pray for you to get saved, God will deal with you and make you miserable."

"How do I do that?" Ken said, looking deep in Annie's eyes.

Annie showed him in her Bible the Romans Road, ending with Romans 10:9–13. Annie said, "You have to pray the sinner's prayer, asking the Lord to forgive you and come into your heart. I will pray it line by line and then you pray it, if you mean it. Lord I have sinned against you, please forgive me. Please come into my heart and save me and take me to Heaven when I die." Annie prayed and Ken repeated her.

Annie said to Ken, "Now, are you forgiven and saved?"

"I believe I am," Ken said smiling. "Now, do you want me to leave?"

"I want you to know you are forgiven," Anne said, opening her arms.

He hugged her and hugged her and whispered, "I should have confessed to you four years ago."

"No, I probably would have not been spiritually able to handle it four years ago."

"Thank you, Annie. I love you."

"God has given me a powerful love for you, Ken. When I was a teenager, I asked God to give me a man to marry I could love with all my heart. God has done just that; you are that man. I need not warn you, though, you need to not think that my forgiveness gives you a license to sin and hurt me again. It is one thing to make a mistake, another to deliberately look for opportunities to sin."

Ken answered, "I don't ever want to hurt you again. I'll be extra careful about being around women. You are precious to me. I don't ever want to lose you."

CHAPTER 19

MANY SUNDAYS CAME and went and Ken still would not go to church. Annie could tell he was a happier person since that night he prayed. They talked about his relationship with Hilda at work. Ken said she was staying away from him. He caught her in the lunchroom one day and apologized to her and told her Annie knew of his flirtations and had forgiven him. Annie was so happy she forgot all about what he confessed to her. God took it away. She realized how easy it was to forgive when you allowed the Lord to have his way in your life.

Annie told Pastor West that she had talked with Ken about salvation, showing him the scriptures, and that he had prayed the sinner's prayer. He still didn't come to church, so Annie asked Pastor West and Mary over for dinner one night. She asked him to share the scriptures with Ken. Pastor West said he would.

Pastor and Mary came and he talked to Ken. Ken listened, but nothing seemed to be hitting his heart. A heart change should have happened had he really been sincerely saved. She didn't give up hope. Pastor West came to the house several times in the next few weeks. Ken and he were getting along well.

One evening, about a month after Ken's confession, he came home from work and told Annie he quit his job. Annie knew it was better for them as a family but also knew the large cut in income meant she would have to go back to work.

"Randy will start building swimming pools again now that summer is here," he told Annie. "I will work with him again."

"If that's what you want, Ken, there is a few hundred dollars in our checking account that will get us by until I find work again. My unemployment will run out soon."

When summer was gone, Ken would be out of work again. Annie got some temporary jobs through a placement agency. This helped out, but Annie knew there had to be more money coming in soon. She made it a matter of prayer.

Ken still wouldn't go to church, so Annie continued taking Sarah and Kenny by herself. Kenny showed an interest in playing the piano. Ken found a lady that really played well. She said she would give him a few lessons. Annie found out the teacher had played for Jack Van Impe at the Crusades for Christ in Detroit. Kenny caught on quickly. Annie realized that how a person plays the piano depends on the teacher. Each teacher has their own touch.

Pastor West was promoting missions and decided to have a missions fair. Several families would take a booth and the best booth would get a prize. A donation jar would be at the door of the fellowship hall to give to the missionaries. Kenny and Sarah wanted to take a table to decorate.

They chose Rural Bible Missions. This was a group of young people who drove around the countryside and held vacation Bible school in rural churches. The group had run VBS last summer at their church. They drove a school bus to the different churches where they were conducting VBS. They used the bus to pick up children and take them to the VBS sessions at the church. Kenny wanted to build a bus with his erector set. Ken helped him make the bus, while Sarah and Annie made artwork to go along with the theme.

The time for the demonstrations of the projects came up and Annie asked Ken, "Will you please come to church tonight and see the missionary projects? Everyone will vote for the best one and then there will be prizes."

Ken said again, "No, not this time. I hope you all win. The Dallas Cowboys are playing tonight on the TV."

"Well, God can't compete with the Cowboys; we will be back around eight. I love you," Annie said, giving Ken a kiss goodbye.

As people were browsing around the table, Mary came up to Annie and said, "How are things going with Ken?"

"He is acting more like a family man, but still no sign of faith in God. I get very discouraged sometimes. Strange thing happened; he bought me a new Bible for our eleventh anniversary last month. I can't help but wonder why my prayers are not answered."

Mary put her arm around Annie's shoulders and said, "Sometimes God is working on us to draw us closer to Him. We want to have our prayers answered, but there might be something He is doing to help us grow to be able to handle the results of our prayers."

"Oh, I know I have grown in my faith and prayer life in the past couple years and got rid of some bad habits. What else might be hindering me?"

"Well, it could be anything: a poor attitude, unforgiving spirit, or some other unconfessed sin that our Lord is trying to show you. We must learn to trust Him through good and bad. We must learn to walk closer to our Lord, so that we can learn to love Him with a deeper love. Listen for His still, small voice."

"I got baptized last year at the same time Kenny did because the church I was saved in did not believe in immersion for baptism. I can see how God led me to do that and I have asked him to forgive me. I have never lost the faith that Ken will be saved soon."

A gavel sounded and Pastor said, "We have a winner. Our blue-ribbon family winner tonight is the Jenkins family with their display of Rural Bible Missions."

Kenny and Sarah were so excited. Annie took a picture of them by the display. They all hurried home. Kenny ran in the house.

"Look, Daddy, a blue ribbon. Thank you for helping me. We won! Isn't that great, Daddy?"

"Yes, son. I am proud of all of you," Ken said as he hugged the kids. "Now, time to scoot on to bed."

Annie picked up a letter and said, "Ken, did you read this letter from your mother that came in the mail yesterday?"

"Yes, I just read it while you were at church."

"Who is Michael Sims?"

"Michael is my cousin from south Georgia. His mother and my mother are sisters. I don't remember much about him. She wants us to look him up. He has recently moved to Pontiac to go to college."

Annie said, "Leave the letter on the table. I'll get a letter out to the address your mother sent and see if I can find out more about him."

"Okay, you do that. Let's go to bed. I have to get up early and get to the construction site where Randy is building that house."

"Did the Cowboys win?" Annie asked.

"They always win; they are about as good as the Georgia Bulldogs."

"I love you, Ken."

"I know you do, and I don't deserve you, but I am happy as long as I can go to bed with you at my side every night."

"Good night, honey."

As Ken lay there sleeping, Annie thought about what Mary said to her. Was there something she had in her life that she had not given to God? She knew God gave her the grace to forgive Ken; she had put his sins completely behind her. Did she have the wrong attitude? She didn't think that was a problem. What could it be? Some unconfessed sin, Mary had said. Her mind went back to the time when she first met Ken. She had fallen so head over heels in love with him that she couldn't think straight.

When Ken left on furlough to go home to Georgia before he went to Korea, Annie went to a work camp with the church teens in Kentucky for two weeks. They repaired things around the church in Kentucky. Annie even learned how to trowel cement poured to make sidewalks for the church. They cooked their own meals, taking turns on kitchen duty. She enjoyed most the experience of being with some stronger spiritual teens than she was at the time. Every night a young man who was a sophomore in a Bible college led devotions. Samuel had a way of penetrating hearts. One night Samuel asked Annie if she was going to go to a Bible college. Annie said, "No, my boyfriend and I plan to marry when I graduate next year."

"Is he a born-again Christian?" asked Samuel.

"No, he was raised in another religion, but he has told me he doesn't believe in it. He went to church with me when he was here. He is on his way to Korea for a year."

"Oh, Annie, do you know the Bible tells us we are not to be unequally yoked with unbelievers? If you go against God's warning, you will have a miserable marriage and no guarantee that he will ever get saved."

Tears rolled down Annie's cheek as she remembered back to that warning. Also her pastor had told her he could not perform the marriage ceremony because Ken was not a born-again Christian. All of a sudden it came to her. *How can I get my prayers answered when I was the one who shut my eyes and heart to God and married Ken anyways? Lord, please forgive me for not listening to the warnings you gave me and save Ken. Why did it take me almost twelve years of marriage to get to this point? Our selfish natures can really lead us astray.* She slept very peacefully that night. She was sure God heard her and would answer her prayers.

The next day she called Becky and told her about her prayer and the letter she got from Ken's mother about Michael.

"Do you know anything about Midwestern College in Pontiac, Michigan? That's where Michael goes to college. Could it be one of those false religion colleges?" she asked Becky.

"Annie, this is perfect. I have a friend that goes to Emmanuel Baptist Church in Pontiac. It is affiliated with that college; it is a Baptist college, where they train men to be preachers. I don't know how it happened, but that young man is just what you need to help Ken."

"Ken's mother sure doesn't know about that college being Baptist or she would have never told Ken to visit his cousin," Annie said.

When she hung up the phone she got some paper and wrote to Cousin Michael about their family, telling him that she was a born-again Christian but Ken had no church preference. She told him Ken needs to be born again, and that she and church friends were praying for him to be saved.

CHAPTER 20

ANNIE PRAYED ABOUT ways to get Ken involved with church people. It dawned on her one day that Ken enjoyed being with people to talk to about the things he was involved doing. Randy's wife Dot had invited them to their house for supper a couple of times and they all went swimming in their pool. One day at supper, Annie said to Ken, "Do you mind if I invite Randy and Dot for Sunday dinner after church this Sunday?"

"That's a good idea; I'll tell Randy about it at work tomorrow."

"I'll call Dot later in the week to remind her in case Randy fails to tell her."

Dot was happy that Annie called and she and Randy both came about thirty minutes after church.

Annie had put a roast beef in the oven with a whole onion. When she got home, she popped some carrots in the broth and added a little water to simmer and covered it. She had peeled the potatoes ahead and put them on the stove to boil so she could make mashed potatoes. She had made an apple pie the day before. She got the salad ready and Sarah set the table. Annie had taught her to put the fork on the left and the knife and spoon on the right. Annie had Sarah use the new stainless she had gotten from her bank for depositing twenty-five dollars in her secret savings account each week.

After eating dinner, Randy was telling them about the John Birch Society. He and Dot had gone to a church meeting with friends of theirs who belonged to it. The meeting was attended by all Birch members.

Randy said, "The Society was founded by a preacher, inspired by his beliefs that Communism was taking over and it had to be fought. They hold the Constitution in strong regard. They teach that it is the responsibility of every American to vote. Any religious person can join; it's not a particular denomination. You both should come sometime."

Annie thought to herself *This sounds like politics, not so much teaching the grace of God*, but she said, "We will think about it, and I will pray for God's direction. Is anyone ready for dessert? I have apple pie in the oven keeping warm."

"Do you have any cheese to put on top of it?" asked Randy.

"Well, I had planned on asking if you want ice cream with it," replied Annie, "but yes, I have some Colby cheese I can slice."

They all tried the warm pie with some cheese to melt on top. It was new to Ken and Annie.

Ken said, "I really like this."

Dot said, "This is really good apple pie. The crust is exceptional. Did you make it yourself?"

"Yes, I did, Dot. I will be glad to share my secret ingredient."

Randy said, "Secret ingredient? What is it?"

"Well, it has a story that goes along with the recipe."

"We don't have anywhere to get to in a hurry, do we Dot?"

"Okay," Annie said. "Once upon a time..." She laughed. "A few years ago, when I was working at the Italian hors d'oeuvres factory, I met two Polish sisters: Emily and Genevieve. I took breaks in the morning with Emily and the afternoons with Genevieve. Genevieve made a very tasty Polish Kolaczki with raisins and I think poppy seeds. She had brought some to work. I mentioned to Genevieve that Emily said she couldn't make as good a Kolaczki as Genevieve could.

"Genevieve said, 'But she makes such good pie crust and she won't give me the recipe. She taunts me with it at all the family gatherings. Can you find out what she uses?'

"I asked Emily what the big secret was about her pie crust and she told me. 'I have told Genevieve, but she does not believe me.'

"'Well then, tell me,' I said.

"'It's vinegar,' she said. 'I use the regular flour, salt, and shortening like most recipes call for, but before I mix the water in the dough, I stir a tablespoon of vinegar into it.'

"So I tried it, and it worked, and that is the secret ingredient in my pie crust."

Randy said, "Wait a minute, did you tell Genevieve the secret?"

"Yes, I did, but she just said, 'Oh, Emily is just telling you that because she knows you are telling me. She won't ever give me that recipe.'

"I excused myself to the bathroom and had to laugh out loud. I get a chuckle every time I think about that experience, and, to top it off, I learned to make a pretty good pie crust."

A little later, Dot said, "Let me help you wash the dishes."

"That won't be necessary; Kenny and Sarah will wash the dishes today."

After Randy and Dot said their goodbyes, Ken took Annie in his arms and said, "You deserve a big kiss for that meal. It was really good."

"I'll take one of those kisses anytime I can get it. Would you like me to invite Becky and Dan and their boys next Sunday?"

"I wouldn't mind a bit," Ken said. "I enjoyed myself today."

The next Sunday, Becky and Dan came in right after church. Annie had a meatloaf and potatoes in the oven, so she put the dinner together pretty quickly.

As they were leaving Dan said to Ken, "The *Billy Graham Crusade* will be on the TV tonight. Maybe you would like to turn it on and watch it."

"I don't know about that, Dan. Usually there is a football game on I like to watch."

Dan went on. "I was sitting at home one night and flipped the channel to a *Billy Graham Crusade* and I was saved that night. At Graham's invitation, I received the Lord as my Savior."

Annie walked them to the door as they left and said, "Thanks for that testimony, Dan. It adds some more testimony to the things Ken has already heard."

"Dinner was good, Annie. See you at church," Becky said.

"We enjoyed your company, Becky. Bye for now."

The next Sunday Pastor West and Mary and the kids came over.

Annie made a roast. Ken did not seem stressed that the pastor was there. He was adjusting to his company.

"Annie, have you ever been to the Grande Bible and Book Store near Detroit?" Mary asked.

"Becky took me there once when we went Christmas shopping in Detroit. That was a great place to visit."

Ken asked, "What is it?"

"It is a whole city block of rooms with Sunday school supplies, visual aids, maps, films, Bibles, and books," said Pastor West. "The kids love it too."

"I just love it," Annie said.

After they had eaten, Pastor West and Mary thanked them for the meal and left because he had to study his message for that night.

Annie knew the Lord was working, providing fellowship with Christians.

CHAPTER 21

ANNIE HAD BEEN up early that Saturday morning washing the clothes and had already hung a load of towels and sheets on the line. The clothes that she was taking out of the agitator now and putting through the wringer into the rinse water were the cotton shirts, blouses, and other light clothes. She had just thrown the jeans and work clothes in the agitator tub and was headed to the lines outside to hang the second load when Ken pulled in the driveway. He had to help Randy finish a job that morning.

When she got back in the house, she said, "You are just in time for breakfast. I wanted to get that second load out to dry before I finished. Sausage patties are ready and I just have to pour the batter to make the pancakes and breakfast will be ready. I hear the kids playing so they apparently are awake."

"How soon will you be done with the washing?" Ken asked.

"After I empty the washer and hang the clothes. I would guess about an hour. Why do you ask?"

"I thought we could all take a ride somewhere nice that you would like to go."

"Okay. What about the Grande Bible and Book Store in Detroit?"

"If you all can be ready to go in an hour, we will go there," Ken said.

Annie ran over and gave Ken a kiss. "Thank you."

"Okay, Kenny and Sarah, you wash the dishes and clear the table while I finish the wash," said Annie as she headed to the washroom.

"It is a windy day so the first two loads are already dry. I folded them and brought them in the house. It won't hurt to leave the jeans on the line," Annie said as she came in the door with a load of clothes. "Let me put my shopping clothes on and I will be ready."

Annie came out in a skirt and blouse and had combed her hair and put some lipstick on. She saw Michael Sims's latest letter on the coffee table and stuck it in her purse. He had written a letter and given his testimony of how he was saved out of a false religion and now was following the Lord by being at a Bible college. He and his wife had surrendered to the foreign mission field. They had two boys, both a little younger than Sarah. They would be happy for them to visit sometime in Pontiac.

"I am so amazed at how lovely you look even without a bunch of that makeup I see other women wear," Ken said as he held Annie's sweater for her to slip on and then kissed her cheek.

"Thank you, tall, dark, and handsome," smiled Annie.

Ken's pat answer to Annie's compliments came. "Unreal."

"Kids, do you have some books, or something to entertain yourself? Detroit is a long ways to go."

"Yes, Mama," Sarah and Kenny said.

The ride to Detroit was uneventful. The kids sat in their seats reading or playing with toys. They knew their dad would not tolerate messing around when he was driving. They were very obedient children, especially when their dad was there.

When they arrived at the Grande Bible and Book Store, Ken said, "Wow, this is big. How long will you be?"

"I could spend the day but I will keep it down to an hour," Annie reassured him.

"I will look around outside and come in and get you in an hour."

"Okay," said Annie. She knew Ken wanted to smoke a cigarette so she went on in with the children.

"Okay, children, these two rooms to our left are filled with things you kids will be interested in; I will be in the main part of the store. If you need me just stand by the door of the room and I will see you and come to you. You may both pick out books or toys or whatever is there that costs no more than three dollars. Don't leave these two rooms."

The kids looked in the rooms and said, "We won't. Wow!"

Annie looked at the visual aids and some of the flannelgraph books. Then she saw some books by Ethel Barrett. Mrs. Barrett was the featured speaker the previous year at the Michigan Sunday School Convention at Cobo Hall in Detroit. She also taught some sessions about storytelling. At Cobo Hall she captured the audience of adults at a banquet for a good hour, telling the story of Cyrus and how he was prophesied to be the one who would set the Jewish people free after they had been in captivity for seventy years. Annie picked up two of her paperback books. One was *There I Stood in All My Splendor* and her newest one out, *Will the Real Phony Please Stand Up?* Annie was delighted to get them at the price of ninety-five cents each. She had decided not to spend over ten dollars.

When she went to get the kids, they were still looking. Just then Ken came in the door and she could see he was looking around, so she waved her hand at him. He came up and said, "Is everyone ready to go?"

"Okay, kids, Daddy is ready to go. Let's go to the counter and pay the cashier for our items."

Sarah and Kenny had picked out two books each. Sarah had also picked out a kit that had a piece of cloth with a Bible verse on it. There was also embroidery thread and needles in it. Annie paid for the items and gave the bag to Kenny to carry. "Looks like Sarah wants some embroidery lessons," Annie said, smiling at Sarah.

As they went to the car, Ken said, "I can see why you like to come here. You know you were in there almost two hours? I never have seen so many different Bibles in one place."

"Yes, I love it. Ken, how close to Utica are we?" Annie said.

"Oh, it is not far. Why? Oh, I know. The Sveden House is there."

"Yaa!" came from the back seat.

"Okay, we will go to the Sveden House."

"You are so sweet," Annie said, smiling. She knew that would be a treat for all of them, including Ken. "I am going to have some glorified rice."

The trip to the Sveden House was another wonderful meal just like the time they went before. As everyone got back in the car, Annie said, "Do we have to go back by the freeway? It is only six o'clock."

Ken said, "Well, it's not far to Pontiac. We could go home that way.

Matter of fact, we could try to find Michael's address. I don't know the number of the apartment, but I went by that street he said he lived on when I worked at the auto factory."

"I have his letter in my purse; I'll see what the return address is on the envelope."

All the way to Pontiac Annie was praying and the most overwhelming faith came to her. It was like God came down and said to her, "Today is the day Ken will be saved."

When they got to the apartment building, Ken got out of the car and said, "Looks like they live upstairs. I will check and make sure they are home."

A few minutes later, Annie saw Ken beckon to her to come upstairs. She got the kids out and showed them where the stairs were going up to the apartment.

"Hello, I am Michael Sims, and you must be Ken's better half," he said, smiling. "Come in and meet the family. This is my wife Pam and my boys, David and Henry."

"Hello. You boys are younger than our kids, but I am sure you will get along."

Pam gave Annie a hug. "Good to meet you after reading the letters you sent."

"I hope we are not interfering with your supper. We have already eaten."

"No, we have already cleaned the kitchen and I was about to pour a glass of sweet tea. Would y'all like some?"

Pam's Southern accent was very noticeable.

"None for me, but Ken probably would like some sweet tea; I wouldn't mind a glass of water." Annie could see Ken and Michael had already sat down in the kitchen talking. Michael's Bible was lying there next to him on the table.

Pam said, "Let's go in the living room and leave the two men alone, and we can get better acquainted."

"Good idea," said Annie.

When they sat down on the couch in the living room, Pam said, "We need to leave them alone in the kitchen. Michael will be sharing his faith with Ken."

"When Ken said he would see if he could find where you lived, I told him I had the address in my purse. I knew as if God was sitting in the car with me that tonight would be the night Ken would get saved."

"Let's pray," said Pam. As they both prayed about what was going on in the kitchen, Annie felt peace.

The ladies conversed back and forth about the kids and how they got here from southern Georgia. Annie knew she liked this lady. Time had slipped by and Annie looked at her watch. An hour had passed by. She could tell things got quieter in the kitchen.

Finally, Ken and Michael came into the living room. Annie could see Ken had some tears in his eyes. Then he said, "I just asked the Lord into my heart and got saved."

Annie jumped up and put her arms around him and hugged him real hard. "That makes me so happy. Michael, thank you so much for leading him to the Lord."

"Well, he was a tough nut to crack," Michael said.

Ken said, "I had heard about Hell in the Bible. I thought it would not be so bad to go to Hell, because my buddies would be there and we could drink and do whatever we wanted. We would have a ball. Michael took me all through that Bible showing me verses I never saw before. Then he showed me the verses in Revelation about death and Hell, being cast into the Lake of Fire. I thought to myself, 'Hell is not so bad, but I don't think I want to go to that Lake of Fire.' Michael explained how Jesus Christ came to die for my sins so that I wouldn't have to go there. He takes the sins and puts them in the deepest sea and remembers them no more. I liked that idea too. So I sincerely prayed the sinner's prayer and I felt the Holy Spirit come into my body."

"And if you don't feel like it tomorrow, you know the Bible says, 'Whosoever calls upon the Lord shall be saved,'" said Michael.

"Yes, I will never be the same again. Now we need to get the kids and get on home. We have to go to church tomorrow," said Ken.

Annie got a tissue and wiped the tears from her eyes. She felt so blessed. Ken had called the kids into the living room and was telling them that they had a new father. He had been saved.

Sarah and Kenny hugged their daddy. "God answered our prayers."

On the way home the kids fell asleep and Ken said, "Annie, I need to call Pastor West as soon as we get home to tell him that I will be walking the aisle to make a public profession of my salvation."

"That's great, Ken."

"Honey, I am so glad you didn't give up on me," Ken said. "I told you I loved you when I married you, but it doesn't even compare for the love I have for you now. If it wasn't for you, I would have gone on in my life not knowing the Lord and would have spent eternity in the awful place called Hell. I sure picked out the best when I chose you."

When they got home, Ken called Pastor West; he was elated about Ken's salvation. Then Ken called his dad in Georgia. Ken said, "I just got saved. I asked the Lord into my heart." Annie could hear though Ken had the phone on his ear. His dad said, "Well, Hallelujah!"

Ken went on and told his dad how it happened. Annie knew Ken's dad did not go to the false church but had no idea he would be happy about Ken's news.

CHAPTER 22

THE NEXT MORNING, Annie got the kids up and breakfast ready. Ken came out of the bedroom all dressed up with a tie and white shirt. Annie's heart felt so full. He was really going to church together with them.

"Do you kids see what a handsome man just came out of my bedroom?"

"Oh, really?"

"Yes, you look really sharp. Come and have some coffee and breakfast."

That morning, as they walked in to sit in the pews together, people turned their heads to see Ken Jenkins attending services on Sunday morning.

Pastor West preached a great sermon on salvation. At the invitation, Ken walked up the aisle and shook hands with Pastor West, repeating what he said the night before. He had received the Lord as his Savior. Pastor West turned toward the audience and said, "Ken Jenkins received the Lord last night. He has come forward to make a public profession of his salvation."

After closing prayer, Becky and Dan had come to congratulate Ken as well as Dot, Randy's wife. Mrs. Cook came up later and said, "Mr. Jenkins, so glad you came to know the Lord."

Mary had Sunday dinner ready and invited the Jenkins to eat with them. After dinner, Ken said, "Pastor, I need to get baptized now. When will that happen?"

"Well, we don't have a baptismal tank at our church. We usually go to a neighboring church. I'll check with them and find out when we can borrow their tank. The important thing is that you are saved from your sin by the blood of Jesus Christ."

Annie said, "I was so happy for Ken to follow through and make his salvation public. I thought more of the people at church would have congratulated him."

"This church has not had an adult walk the aisle and make a public profession in a long, long time. I have been praying for the congregation because I don't see the fruits of salvation in many of them. Ken, your stepping out to do the right thing was a good beginning. We will have to wait and see what happens next."

As they walked home together, Kenny said, "Does this mean you will go to church with us every Sunday, Daddy?"

"Yes. Kenny and Sarah, I make you a promise with Jesus as my Lord, you have a new daddy who plans to go to church every time the doors are open to me."

Ken called his mother after dinner. "Mom, I wanted you to know that I made public this morning in church giving testimony of my salvation experience and that I was saved for all eternity. If anything happens to me, I will go right to Heaven."

A pause while his mother said something.

"I did not believe in that religion then and I don't believe it now," he said. "I will talk to you later. I need to hang up now."

When he hung up the phone Annie said, "What did she say?"

"She said I was baptized into her church when I was twelve years old and I will always be a member."

Annie hugged Ken and said, "I'm sorry she gave you a hard time."

"No surprise to me. I expected her to say something like that."

"Honey, I have prayed so long for you to be saved. Many times I became discouraged with your actions but Pastor and Mary along with Becky and Dan encouraged me with their prayers. I thought you were saved when you prayed the sinner's prayer for me that one night. I knew you weren't when you wouldn't go to church. I saw no change."

Ken said, "I so wanted forgiveness from you, I would have done anything you told me. I know you tried to show me I needed forgiveness from God, but I was just thinking about you. I couldn't understand why I did such awful things to you. The terrible guilt from those sins was dragging me down for so long. Now I know the difference. I got the forgiveness from God and Jesus Christ is now my Savior. I will ever be grateful to you that you didn't give up on me. I promise to never knowingly hurt you again."

"I kept trusting God that he would send you the right person to help you understand. Who would have thought God would send your cousin from southern Georgia all the way up to Pontiac, Michigan, so that you could be saved? God works in mysterious ways. If your mother knew why Michael was here, she never would have given us his address and told us to look him up."

"That trip to the Grande Bible and Book Store was you trying to get me to Michael's. You were being devious," Ken said.

"No, it really wasn't. I wanted to get you to Michael, but that was God who put it in your mind to go through Pontiac, not mine."

"I love you so much, Annie. I didn't know such ability to love before I knew the Lord."

Tears ran down Annie's face and all she could say was, "Thank you, Jesus."

Michael called to check up on Ken to see if he followed through. While he was on the phone he invited them to come to the college church Monday or Tuesday night because they were having a soul-winning conference.

They took the children and went Monday night. There were over three thousand people at the conference. Ken and Annie had never seen that many people in church before that day. At invitation there were about twenty people who went forward to be saved. They were so enthused by the preaching that Annie invited Becky and her husband to go with them Tuesday. The same thing happened; another large group of people saved. This encouraged Ken in his new faith. The preaching on soul winning made them all more soul conscious.

A couple months later, Pastor West found a church baptismal tank for Ken's baptism. Ken said the water was freezing when they put him under, but he didn't mind because he was finally baptized.

In the next few days, Ken gave a testimony to all his friends and workmates. He was very vocal. That slowed their friendships. They weren't asking him to go places with them any longer. Ken and Annie stayed busy with their friends at church and soul winning.

Most of the people at the church did not care for Ken's zeal, especially the men he had drank with at the bars. Ken told Annie he could not understand why people did not try to win others to the Lord. One Sunday, when Michael and family had come to visit Annie and Ken's church, Ken talked to Michael about the problem.

"Why don't you start a new church with the people who want to win souls?"

"How would I do that?"

"First you need to let the pastor know what you have in mind, so he won't be upset with you for taking people from his church. I can talk to Dr. Malone about finding you a preacher. Then you have to find a building for a church."

When Ken talked to Pastor West, the pastor said, "It would not upset me at all. I have been talking to God about doing a different ministry because the people at this church are not following me. They do what they want to do. The deacons try to tell me how to preach and they hate the fact that we are trying to win people to the Lord."

Annie said, "But Pastor, if you leave you won't have a place to live and no finances. What will you and your family do?"

"Mary has already found a job in town, and I will find something until I find out what the Lord has for me. I think it will be in children's ministry."

Next Ken got in touch with Becky and Dan and told them what they were doing. They in turn talked to Randy and Dot. Randy said they could use the back room of his garage if they wanted to for their church. Things went so fast. Michael gave them the name of an older man who was interested in meeting them along with Dr. Malone. The next Sunday all of Ken's family and all of Dan's family went to Dr. Malone's church. After the services they met with Dr. Malone, who introduced them to one of his deacons, an older man. Brother Paul Garrison had graduated from the Bible college. He was a great soul winner. Brother Garrison was just what they were looking for at their new gathering of people.

Brother Garrison came to the garage that first Sunday and preached. He was a great preacher. He said he would come out to the country to preach and knock on doors with them each weekend if they could find him a place to stay along with his wife, Belinda.

Becky and Dan took alternating weekends with Annie and Ken fixing meals and finding a spare room for the new pastor and his wife. Ken and Annie gave the Garrisons Kenny's bedroom and Kenny slept on the couch.

So plans went on. Ken spent every Saturday out with Pastor Garrison knocking on doors. They got the town drunk saved when he heard Ken's testimony. He had a stroke the next week and died. Ken was relieved to know his former friend would go to Heaven. Everyone was talking about the change in Ken Jenkins. No one was happier than Annie; she thanked God every day for saving her husband and making him a new creature in Christ.

CHAPTER 23

IT WAS A lazy Sunday afternoon and Ken was watching football. Annie sat down beside him and he put his arm around her shoulders like he often did. Annie waited for a commercial and said to Ken, "You know that I have been using birth control since Sarah was born, but you don't know why. It has been because I did not want to raise any more children with a father who wasn't saved. Since things have changed, I would like to know: is it all right with you if I stop the birth control and we have another baby?"

"Right now? The football game is on now; if you wait until halftime I'll be happy to oblige."

Annie started laughing. "Not now silly; I just wanted to know so I could stop taking birth control pills."

Ken smiled at her and said, "I think it would be a great plan."

Shortly after Ken got saved, they had gone to Pennsylvania to visit. Ken gave a testimony to Annie's family of his salvation experience and explained how now he would not go to Hell.

Annie's dad just said, "There is no such place as Hell. A good God would not send anyone to a fiery pit."

No one else had any comments.

About a month later, Annie's sister had written her a letter and asked them not to come to her house for Thanksgiving that year as they usually did because no one wanted to hear about their religion.

Annie invited Michael and Pam to their house along with another family from their Georgia church, John and Linda Perry and their two teenage sons, for Thanksgiving dinner. She cooked a big turkey and made Southern cornbread dressing, mashed potatoes, green bean casserole, cranberry sauce, rolls, pumpkin pie, and sweet tea. She had to put a card table at the end of the kitchen table to accommodate everyone.

After dinner the kids all went outside to play. Kenny shared his bike with the older boys. All the adults sat in the living room and got acquainted. Brother Perry was older than Michael and Ken and seemed to have a great wisdom about him. He had sold his house when called to preach, packed up his family, and come to Michigan to Dr. Malone's college.

After they went home Ken said, "I don't know when I enjoyed Thanksgiving as much as I did today. How did you know how to make cornbread dressing?"

"That cookbook I got from the book club had a step-by-step procedure. I have gotten a lot of recipes from it that I have used."

"Well it was great and you deserve an extra kiss for doing so much to make Thanksgiving dinner so good and the people comfortable with Southern foods. I really liked the Perry family."

"Yes, we will have to invite them again. Christian fellowship is just like family."

Pastor Garrison and his wife had found a little apartment over a gas station to stay at on weekends so Annie didn't have a lot of company now.

One night Annie got a call from her brother saying he and his wife and little girl were coming to visit for a few days. That seemed odd to Annie because they had not been there before.

Annie said to Ken, "We must pray for them to be saved. It is not a coincidence that they are visiting us. God must be dealing with some hearts."

Lee and Karen arrived that Friday night with their sweet little girl, Janice. Sarah got along well with Janice; she loved having a little girl to play with her dolls.

Ken called Michael and asked him to come over Saturday to visit, explaining that Annie's brother was not saved and was there visiting.

Next morning, Annie could hear some raised voices in the bedroom that Lee and Karen were in and then it stopped. Lee came out and Annie said, "Do you all want eggs or pancakes for breakfast?"

Lee said, "We are going to get a divorce for breakfast."

A little later Karen came out of the bedroom acting like nothing was wrong so Annie asked her about breakfast.

After breakfast was over, Ken was watching a NASCAR race with Lee. Annie and Karen were talking in the kitchen. Karen told Annie she was about two months pregnant but she was scared because she had lost two babies because of her Rh negative blood type. Annie had not heard of a problem like Karen's. She listened intently to her talk about it.

Annie heard Ken open the door; Michael, Pam, and the boys were here. Introductions were made and Pam came out to the kitchen to visit with the ladies.

When Karen told Pam about the pregnancy, Pam said, "Karen, I have a friend that had that Rh negative problem. Her doctor gave her a shot that is new in treating that condition and she was okay and had a healthy baby."

"Well that is good news; I will have to check with my OB doctor when we go home."

They were discussing their children and enjoying each other's company when Ken called from the living room, "Ladies, come in here."

When they went to the living room, Lee said, "I just asked the Lord to save me and I know I am going to Heaven now when I die. Michael just showed me the way."

Annie said, "That is wonderful, Lee. I am so happy for you."

Michael said, "Karen, are you 100 percent sure you would go to Heaven when you die?"

Karen looked startled but she said, "Yes, I go to the Lutheran church."

Lee continued asking Michael questions. Annie found a Bible for him he could borrow while there. Michael explained to Lee he needed to read that Bible and let God lead him.

Karen and Lee went to church with them the next morning and Lee started reading his Bible starting in Genesis. They stayed a few more days and by the time they left Lee had read through the Old Testament. Pastor Garrison told him to get in church when he went home. He told him to look for a church that had buses to pick up kids. You will know they care for people.

When Lee and Karen got home, Karen wrote what a great caring people they found at the church. Lee was going knocking on doors with the pastor. She had gone to her doctor and gotten the new shot for her condition. It made Annie's heart so happy.

A couple of months later Annie found out she was pregnant. She had been working part-time jobs and knew she did not want to get a permanent job when she had the baby. She got a job at the county office that was to last four months. She used an adding machine verifying tax rolls in the townships and cities in that county.

Ken came in one night and said that the landlord had raised the rent. It was up to seventy-five dollars now, but that was the first raise since they lived there. He also mentioned that Randy had told him about a house in the city that was being sold reasonably. Maybe they could buy it.

"Let's find out more about it," said Annie.

They met the realtor the next Saturday. "The house payment is only $15 a month, but you will have to come up with $1,000 down. The man who owns it will take a land contract for $10,000 at 8 percent interest," said the realtor. "Here we are. I'll unlock the door."

"I don't know where we could get the down payment," said Ken.

"Let's look at it before we talk money," said Annie.

"It has a basement, with a natural-gas furnace that was a coal furnace before they converted it to gas," the realtor said. "Let's go down and check it out."

"There is a pool table down here," exclaimed Ken.

"You see that chute above the table? That comes from the bathroom and puts the dirty clothes down here, where your washer goes."

"Neat; I like that idea," said Annie.

"The basement looks solid," Ken said. "Okay, there is only one bedroom on the main floor. Let's look at the upstairs."

Annie walked up the stairs and said, with a disappointed look on her face, "It is one big attic room."

"That's nothing to worry about, honey; I could partition off a room for Sarah and leave the rest for the boys."

Annie looked at Ken and said, "What boys?"

"Kenny and his new baby brother," Ken replied. "I am going to name him after Tom Malone."

Annie had not told Ken, but she prayed and told the Lord if he would give her a boy, she would raise him the best she knew how to be a preacher.

Annie said, "If you can make Sarah a room and remodel the kitchen to put some cupboards in it, paint the outside and inside, then I will come up with the down payment. I like the idea of living in our own home."

"When do you need the down payment, Mr. Smith?" Ken asked.

"We can set up the closing in a couple days. We will need it then."

"Christmas break will be here next week," Annie said, "and the kids can change schools when they go back in January. We will live closer to my work here also, so what do you say Ken?"

"You never cease to amaze me, Annie. I say yes."

After the realtor left Ken said, "Annie, where are you going to get that money?"

"While I was working for the hospital equipment company, I put $25 in the bank each week, and also when you were working at the car factory. That's how I got the new stainless flatware for free that we have been using recently. If I calculate right, I have the $1,000. That will cover the down payment and probably leave another $200 for remodeling. Let's pray about it and go check the balance at the bank; it is just a couple miles down the street."

After Ken prayed he drove toward the bank. On the way, Ken saw a body shop that had a "Help Wanted" sign out. He said, "Annie, can you go to the bank and pick me up on the way back?"

Annie waited to make sure someone was inside the body shop since it was Saturday. Then she went on to the bank. She had the cashier give her a cashier's check for the $1,000 and withdrew $200 cash for the remodeling that she tucked away in the secret compartment of her wallet.

She pulled in the driveway of Bob's Body Shop and got out of the car. She opened the door and saw Ken and a man talking. When they saw Annie, the man came and introduced himself. "I am Bob, and I own this shop that your husband is going to work at starting Monday."

"Oh great, I am Annie. I am glad to meet you," she said, shaking his hand. Annie could see the shop was small, but there were three cars in it, partially fixed.

On the way home, Ken said, "I talked him into hiring me. I told him I had done a little body work with cars at the gas station. He said he would start me at two dollars an hour but increase it if I could do the work. I am sure I can do it; you won't have to worry."

"Honey, we have been praying for a job that would give you something that you liked to do. I am sure God will reward you. It is only about a mile from our new house. The house payments are only fifteen a month. That is saving sixty dollars. I am all for it."

She showed the $1,000 cashier's check to Ken. He squeezed her hand. "God is so good to me. He answers our prayers. I can't praise him enough. I wish I had listened to him sooner than I did so we wouldn't have had to go through so much heartache."

CHAPTER 24

KEN LOVED WORKING at Bob's Body Shop. Bob doubled his pay after the first week. Annie was so thankful to the Lord for finding Ken work that he loved to do. Bob let him work on Saturdays on anything he wanted to since Bob's business was closed. Ken had bought an old wrecked van and fixed it up for a total cost of thirty-five dollars.

Baby Tom was born. Ken had been right that the boys' room needed to be the larger one. Annie was delighted and she knew God would answer the rest of her prayer: that this baby boy would become a preacher someday. She told no one and planned to never tell about this promise until the boy was called by God. Ken remodeled the house, putting the new cupboards in and sectioning a room out for Sarah in the upstairs area.

Ken took the family in the van he had fixed up to see the locks in the Upper Peninsula. It was interesting for Annie to see how the ships went in the lock from the higher lake, Lake Superior. When the water was let out, the ship was in the lower lake, Lake Huron. The Sault Ste. Marie International Bridge connected the cities Sault Ste. Marie in Michigan with Sault Ste. Marie, Ontario, Canada. It is 2.8 miles long. Ken took them across it and turned around and came right back. They all had a picnic lunch and then went on across the Upper Peninsula through Wisconsin's tip and into Minnesota, where Annie's brother Russell lived. Ken gave his testimony of his newfound faith, but it didn't seem to faze Russell. It was a fun vacation, not the same trip to Georgia every summer.

In the meantime, the church had grown past the capacity for the back garage room to handle. The men of the church went to the bank to get a loan to build a church.

Randy had given the church five acres behind the garage. The church savings account showed that they had $10,000 to start. The bank wanted three men who owned property to sign the loan for the building. All the people were elated that they would be in a building. The men said they would help build it. They had been in this garage church for a year.

Ken left early Saturday morning to help with the pouring of cement. Around nine he called Annie and said, "Pastor and I are the only ones who showed up to trowel this cement. The first truck left and there will be several more. I am desperate, but could you please come and help?"

"I certainly will try; my teenage work camp experience may come in handy."

She saw the cement truck leaving just as she got there. She grabbed a trowel, saw a place that needed smoothing out, and got right to it. When they got through with the cement work, Annie's back hurt from the bending over. About that time Becky came up with some sandwiches and lemonade.

"Sorry Dan wasn't able to help; he had to work."

"Thanks for bringing the sandwiches," Pastor Garrison said. He looked tired.

That night Annie asked Ken, "What is next on the building?"

"The framing needs to be put up next."

He continued, "We have to get a framer. The men can help, but we need someone who knows what they are doing. Just as I was talking to you, I thought of someone. I fixed his work truck when he had a wreck."

Ken called the framer and he said he would talk to the men.

"Lewis, the framer, met with the men of the church. He gave them an estimate. He starts this week," Ken said to Annie the next night. "He is telling the lumber yard what we need and our treasurer will send them a check."

It took about four months to get the building up. Ken was working every Saturday on the building. Annie was so happy to see her husband so excited about doing something for the Lord. Ken's faith was real. He was still witnessing to people.

The church held two hundred people. There were fifty people now to dedicate the church. Ken and Annie sang in the choir and duets together. Ken's beautiful voice that used to sing Elvis's love songs to Annie was now singing hymns. Ken had thrown his Elvis albums in the trash except for the one where Elvis sang hymns.

The men who graduated from Dr. Malone's college were called his preacher boys because he trained them. There were several of these churches around the area. The teenagers went once a month to visit one of Dr. Malone's preacher boys' churches for youth rallies. They had music, Bible quizzes, preaching, and great fellowship for teens. Ken volunteered to drive the Sunday school bus bringing in the people who didn't have a ride to church. He drove the bus to the teen rallies also.

Annie and Becky went out on Tuesday mornings knocking on doors to find people who did not attend church. A family they met had five kids. They had just moved there. The lady said they were saved and had just moved there from Pennsylvania for the husband's job. Annie had a lot to talk to them about, since she had lived in Pennsylvania in her younger days. Doris and Jonathan Patterson came Sunday morning. They all joined the church. The next week they brought Doris's brother and his wife that lived next door.

One Tuesday morning, they knocked on a door and met a young lady who had been crying. Becky talked to Sylvia and found out she had just had a fight with her husband and really wanted to leave him. Annie asked her if the pastor could come and talk to them both Saturday. She agreed. After talking with the pastor she and her husband were both in church Sunday morning. Ken had gone with Pastor and given his testimony. Both had received the Lord when Pastor talked to them. Her husband Paul was a welder. When he found out the church didn't have a baptismal tank yet, he told the pastor he would make one and install it. No payment necessary. In praying for a way to get a baptismal tank, who would guess that four people following the Lord's path for them would not only get people saved but a baptismal tank.

Ken and Pastor Garrison visited together on Saturday morning. Everyone was talking about the miracle church. More people who were already saved came, but just about once a month someone received the

Lord and made a public profession. The Lord was blessing the work of the people. The attendance was up, running about eighty each Sunday.

Revival was coming up next week. Everyone was anxious to have this meeting. In the meantime, Annie heard from her mother that she was coming to visit for a week. One of the ladies of the church talked to her and showed her the gospel message. She asked the Lord to save her. She went forward at the revival meeting, made a public profession, and got baptized in the new tank.

Saturday after the revival, Ken said, "Seeing your family come to the Lord burdens me more about my family."

"I still have a sister and a brother who are not saved. I will keep praying for them as well as your family."

A knock at the door sent Ken to answer it. Annie could hear Ken talking and realized it was some elders from Ken's mother's church affiliation. She heard one say they were from Sarnia, Canada, because they did not have a church in the Maysville area. Ken invited them in to sit down.

Annie thought, *He better not go out that back door and leave me with these elders like he used to.*

Ken said, "Gentlemen, I want to tell you that about two years ago I became a Christian by asking the Lord Jesus Christ in my heart. I do not now nor never have I had an interest in your religion."

"Are you saying that you do not believe that our leader is perfect in knowledge and understanding of God's revelation and is a prophet?"

"I don't believe in your leader, if that is what you are asking."

"We will be on our way then," the elder replied.

The next week Ken got a letter in the mail from the false church. It said that Ken had rejected Jesus Christ and so was excommunicated from the church. It angered Annie because nothing was asked about believing in Jesus Christ, and besides, Ken started off with a testimony that he had come to know the Lord Jesus Christ. Ken just brushed it off. "I am through with them; I don't care about their letter. They won't be back."

The next time they went to visit his family in Georgia, Ken gave the letter to his mother.

She read it and said, "This can't be true."

Ken told her exactly what happened, making sure she understood it was the leader he denounced, not the Lord.

She got down on her knees. "No son, don't say that. He is a true prophet."

"I am done with that church. They won't be back to bother me. Do what you want with the letter. I am a born-again Christian now. I have no use for that religion."

On the way home from Georgia, Ken said, "I had a private conversation with my dad. I told him since I was saved I needed to tell him I had forgiven him for the abuse he put on me as a child. We both cried and then hugged each other."

"That is great, Ken. You have learned godly forgiveness. I love you," Annie said as she reached up and kissed his cheek. "By the way, I believe we are going to have another baby in seven months."

Ken smiled at Annie. "Another boy. I think I'll name this one after my grandfather, who was a circuit-riding preacher. His name will be Richard."

"What if it is a girl?"

"It won't be a girl, because the upstairs is all set up for boys."

"You are so sure of yourself. Are you happy we are having another child as a companion to play with his or her brother Tom?"

"You bet I am; can't think of anything better to happen to us than to have another boy. Of course, another pretty girl like Sarah would be all right too."

"Tom will be two years old when the baby comes. We don't have any insurance so we will have to do like we did with Tom. We will pay the doctor each visit and skip your vacation to pay for the hospital bill. Or I could work at the county office awhile."

"You only stayed at the hospital overnight. It cost us $250. It will work out the same as it did before; the Lord took care of the cost. I think we can manage without you going back to work. Tom needs you at home. I'll pick up extra work at the shop for Saturdays, and you can sneak it in that special savings account you keep hidden."

Annie said, "I was just thinking back to the time when I had to leave Kenny and Sarah at home when I worked. Oh, how I hated it. It is so great to have a new man to live with, my Christian husband. Everything is new, especially your attitude."

CHAPTER 25

ANNIE AND KEN'S baby was born, and yes, it was another boy. There would be fewer clothes to buy, as he could wear Tom's. Annie dressed him in a one-piece jumper with feet for the nursery at church. One of the teenage girls thought he was the cutest thing and always wanted to babysit him in the nursery. One Sunday he had a white jumper on. She said he looked like the Pillsbury Doughboy and nicknamed him that.

Kenny and Sarah were doing well in school; Kenny still played the piano. He played well enough to substitute if the main pianist was not at church. Sarah had a sweet voice and sang solos.

Ken had heard of a Christian camp in Tennessee where many great preachers came to preach on family weeks. The family went there on vacation and then on to Georgia to visit Ken's family. Ken thoroughly loved the preaching. He was really charged up for the Lord each time they left the camp. This was the second year to visit. When they were in Decatur, they found a great soul-winning church to attend. Spiritually they all were growing and praising the Lord for his grace. Ken had been saved four years. After the trip back home, Ken brought the suitcases in the house and said, "I have to go see Pastor Garrison."

"Why so late? Can't it wait?"

"No, he always stays at the church on Saturday night late. It's important."

When Ken got back, the kids were all in bed. Annie was studying her Sunday school lesson. She loved teaching juniors.

As he came in the house, he said, "Honey, come sit on the couch with me. I have something to say to you."

"This sounds serious. What have I done wrong?"

"Annie, I love you more than I ever thought possible," he said, giving her a kiss. "I have been praying with Pastor Garrison tonight about a big change in our life."

"Change? You really have my attention now."

"I want to move to Decatur to be near my family. You know I have been burdened about their souls. I believe God wants me to move there. Pastor Garrison gave me some good advice. He prayed with me about it. He said I should pray about it for a year, and if I felt the same way, make the plans to move. He said in a couple of months the Pattersons are moving back to Pennsylvania. The Smith family left last week. He said our family leaving the church now would be a big hindrance on the work here."

"One year? Have you thought this through, Ken? You have a job that you thoroughly love, and when he retires, Bob will probably let you buy the shop. He already built the addition on the building you suggested. He says he is making more money than he ever did before you came there to work. Besides, he gives you credit for the hard work you do for him."

"I know that it will be hard for all of us to leave. I sure hope I can find a boss like Bob in Decatur. I know I can work for my dad until I find something in body work. But all in all, I feel God's hand in this just as if he were talking to me audibly."

"Ken, you are the man I married and promised to love and obey. I think you know I have always submitted to your authority. I would not go against anything you wanted, even before you got saved. I see in you a new creature God made. I got the great privilege of living with a man who has given his heart, soul, and mind to the Lord. I love you more and more every day. I admit it is scary moving with four children to Decatur, but I agree your family needs a witness. I also know God will provide for us because I have seen him do it before in hard times. I will follow you wherever you say God leads us. I trust you."

"Annie, we both need an assurance that we are doing the right thing. Let's make it a sign from God between us that if the church here has attendance of one hundred people in a year's time, we will move. It's a country church with about seventy-five people now. It will be like the fleece of Gideon. If the church doesn't grow, we will stay here; if it grows to one hundred, we will go to Decatur."

"Yes, good idea. Let's not mention to anyone our plans."

"Agreed. Now I am going to get a shower and get in the bed," Ken said.

"Ken, pray with me about it."

Ken put his arm around Annie and they both bowed their heads. Ken prayed very earnestly to God about the move.

The church had built on a fellowship hall with a kitchen area and several Sunday school rooms the past year. The church family had many dinners in that big room. Annie thought every time she was with the church family, I *will miss them*.

One Sunday a lady and man came in and sat in the back pew. Annie recognized the man as a man who had been divorced several years ago. His wife had been unfaithful to him. This lady looked a few years younger than him. She was pretty with long brown hair down to her waist.

Ken went over and shook his hand after church services. Annie came up to them just to hear Ken say, "Why don't you eat dinner with us? You can stay for church tonight and not drive back to Detroit until after evening services." Then he saw Annie. "This is my wife. Annie, you know Gary. This is his fiancée, Rosalind."

Annie shook hands with Gary and said, "Nice to meet you, Rosalind. I understand you are going to our house for dinner. I hope you like breakfast. Waffles are dinner today."

"That sounds great to me; you are very kind to invite us," Rosalind said.

"Do you want to ride with me to the house with the kids? Ken can ride with Gary." She looked at Ken and said, "If that is okay with you?"

"Sure," he said. Then he whispered in her ear. "Sorry I put you on the spot. I'll make it up to you."

Annie smiled at him.

Annie had learned on the way to the house that Gary had led Rosalind to the Lord on their first date. Rosalind lived in East Detroit where Gary had been visiting his cousin. They had been dating about six months and visiting different churches. Gary lived about eight miles from here, so that is why they tried this church. Rosalind was a bookkeeper like Annie used to be, so they had that in common. Plus, when she got to the house, she realized she loved antiques as Annie did. Annie could see she was a new creature who knew nothing about the Bible, but she had an eagerness to learn.

There was good fellowship at the table. Gary and Rosalind came to church regularly after that first time. They continued going with the Jenkins family to their house for waffles and sausage. They set a date for the wedding. Gary had been building a house for them to live in not far from the church. At a wedding shower for Rosalind held at Annie's house, Rosalind brought Annie a new waffle iron as a hostess gift.

Annie and Becky continued going out knocking on doors. One day they knocked on a farmhouse door. A lady came to the door with a baby in her arms. Annie told her that they came to see if they had a church home. The lady said, "Oh, we go to the Catholic church."

Annie remembered what Pastor had told them: "Catholics think when you ask them if they are saved that we mean baptized." So Annie said, "Have you ever been born again?"

"I don't know what you mean. Come on in and tell me about it."

Angie was her name. Since they were having a revival at church that week, she came to church with her husband and went forward at the invitation. She told the evangelist she had been born again that day and wanted to make it public.

Annie told Ken later, "That was the easiest person I have ever led to the Lord. And they say Catholics are hard to win."

"I don't know if you saw this, but after the service, the pastor led her husband to the Lord."

"Praise the Lord; God is so good."

Angie and Roy were both baptized and joined the church. They became faithful members. Roy asked if there was another bus to drive.

Ken said, "You can ride with me and learn my route and take it over. It goes right by your house."

That was the way that Ken relinquished his bus route. He knew someone needed to take it over someday when they left. It was getting closer to that day. The church was growing again. What a blessing to watch.

Taking Ken's lead, she looked for someone who could take her Sunday school class. She asked Belinda, the pastor's wife, if she would help her out and learn to be her substitute teacher. Belinda knew why she asked and said she would.

When the year was up, the attendance in the church was at an all-time high of 137 people. Annie and Ken knew what that meant. They would have to leave these people that they had learned to love and move to Decatur.

They told their children about the move. The two older ones were all excited. Ken called his family in Georgia to tell them what they were doing. He asked if the basement apartment would be available for a few weeks until they found a house. Of course, his family was excited also about the move.

The house sold for $10,000 more than they had paid for it four years ago. The people would be moving in next week. They said goodbye to their neighbors.

Annie tried to look at the move as a new adventure God was taking them on. She packed everything up. Ken got a rental truck to move furniture and some of the boxes. The church people had given them a farewell dinner after church last Sunday, so they were ready to leave Michigan, the state they had lived in for almost fifteen years.

Annie went through the house one last time with Ken to see if they left anything behind. Ken would drive the truck with Kenny riding with him. Annie would drive the station wagon with the younger children and Sarah, who was a great babysitter.

Ken took her in his arms and kissed her. "Annie, I know this is hard on you. It's one more time that I see the love of God through you. Thank you for not giving up on me. Thank you for putting up with a husband that didn't deserve you. I was so hurtful and unkind to you those first twelve years of our marriage. I believe the Lord has made me a new creature in Christ and he used you to do it. I married you because I loved me and wanted you. When I got born again, I learned that day how very much I loved you. I will try to never let you down again."

"Ken, I have to give God the praise for us. He gave me that beautiful love for you, and that's how I got through those twelve years. It was worth it to spend these past five years living with a new man, this creature in Christ. I love you very much."

Ken said, "Now, let's pray for God's safety and then get these children in the vehicles. God has a great new adventure for us."

Annie knew whatever that adventure was, God would be with them, helping them each step of the way.

The Romans Road Annie uses for winning
others to Christ can work for you also.

Mark your Bible with the Romans Road so that you can be ready to
lead someone to Christ. Read the Scriptures to them, showing them
you are taking it from the Bible. You can memorize everything below so
that you are prepared. If you memorize the scripture, you can hold the
Bible where they can see the verse that you are reading. The following
is what you say to them.

Read I John 5:13 to them and say, "Eternal life is a know-so salvation.
Are you 100 percent sure that if you died today you would go to Heaven?
Not think so or hope so, but do you know for sure? Would you like me
to show you?"

In the margins of your Bible after I John 5:13, write Romans 3:10. This
will lead you to the next verse. This is the only verse not in the book
of Romans. Mark in your Bible after Romans 3:10 the next reference,
which is 3:23. No need to keep writing Romans, because you are staying
in Romans. Do that through all of the following references.

1. A person must know that they are sinners. Romans 3:10
   Why are we not righteous? Because Romans 3:23
   Why are we sinners? We were born that way. Romans 5:12.
   That one man was Adam. Adam and Eve sinned in the Garden
   of Eden and brought death on all mankind.

2. A person needs to know the punishment for sin is Hell. Romans
   6:23. Just tell them in Revelation 20:14 it says death and Hell
   were cast into the lake of fire.
   (If needed, look up and read Revelation 20:14. However, it is
   better to stay in one book in the Bible so as not to confuse the
   one you are talking to.)

3. A person needs to know that Jesus loves them. Romans 5:8 We all deserve to go to Hell but Jesus loved us so much that he paid the price of Hell.

4. A person must believe that Jesus died, was buried, and arose from the dead. Read Romans 10:9–10. "There are only eighteen inches between head knowledge and really being saved. There are eighteen inches from head to heart. I can show you from the Bible that there are two things needed to be saved but you personally have to receive it."
   a. Belief in your heart
   b. Confession with the mouth

At this point, review what you told them.

1. Do you believe that you are a sinner?
2. Do you believe that sinners go to Hell?
3. Do you believe Jesus loves you and wants you to be saved?
4. Do you believe Jesus died on the cross for your sins and paid the penalty for you?
   If you believe that, then the way you receive Jesus in your heart is very simple.
5. To be saved a person must ask. Romans 10:13. Put your own name there and make it personal. For (Annie) shall call upon the name of the Lord (she) shall be saved.

Ask them: "Would you like to ask Him to come into your heart right now?"

Help them to pray a simple prayer and ask them to bow their heads and repeat after you if they really believe it.

"Lord Jesus, I know I am a sinner; I deserve to go to Hell. Please forgive me of my sins. I thank you for dying for me; I believe you arose from the dead. I ask you to come into my heart right now and save me. In Jesus's name, amen."

"Now, if you died today, where would you go?

How do you know that? Because God's word says 'Whosoever shall call upon the Lord shall be saved.'"

If you have received the Lord as your Savior through reading any part of this book, please let the author know.

P.O. Box 223
Millbrook, AL 36054